MW01631918

Love Don't Love Nobody

By Frank Howard

ISBN: 9780578859262

Printed in the United States of America

Dedication

This book was written on behalf of my first heartbreak at a very young age; love or puppy love or thinking you're in love, at least. It was a real true experience, a very key part of my life and the becoming of the genuine person and man I am today. I think we have all been in this situation in our lives and can all relate, whether breaking someone's heart or being on the receiving end of it. At the end of the day, God brought me through it all, and put people and resources I've encountered to help and inspire me.

I would like to dedicate this book to the greatest parents in the world - Ossie and Martha Howard.

One of the best co-workers and friend, Alvarro Santi Gomez.

@Alpha_Male_s for a push to stay on my purpose and finding it.

@payroll_giovanni for my musical push and motivation.

@ShanikaTheWriter for her guidance, help, and brilliant writing skills, making my dream a reality.

All of my friends and family members who supported me when I experienced my heartbreak. I am forever grateful.

God Bless!

Table of Contents

Preface

The heart is more deceitful than all else and is desperately sick. The heart does want what the heart wants, but that's the problem. You can't trust your heart. It only wants all sorts of evil. But that doesn't mean that all is lost. - Jeremiah 17:9

Where do I start? Well, it was January 11, 1999 at 2:38 a.m. I had just gotten off the phone with the one woman I wanted to spend the rest of my life with. I say that it was funny, but it was quite sad because she didn't feel that she was worthy. It always happens that way.

Me, just being the person I am, nothing more, nothing less, I'm just like any other human being--no better than the next man. I'm a man that realizes that nobody is perfect. Everybody has his or her own perception of what a good man is. True enough, I'm only 21 years old, and I'm all man. There's plenty more fish in the sea.

Some people would say that I got my whole life ahead of me. Wrong, because I don't know that...only God knows. True, I'm not suffering from illness, disease, or any other symptoms. As I write this, I could be gone by the next couple of lines, but God chose otherwise. Everything that I'm about to let you in on is because of him. He gave me the gift to do it, so when it is all said and done, if you learn nothing else from me, know this...man, woman, male, female, and human beings are the most imperfect creatures I know. Why? Because I'm one of them and I learned from the experiences that I have had, but it goes beyond that. Everything I say and write, please listen and read closely, because one minute you will think it is good, then it only gets better.

Chapter 1 - My Weekend Out
(The Road to Rap)

It was a typical weekend, summer of 1998 - small town, small world where everybody basically knows everybody. In my world, nobody knows what won't hurt him or her. Shoot, I'm only 20 years old and I've accomplished a whole hell of a lot than people that's 30, 35, 50, or maybe even 55 years old. But that don't make me no better than anybody else, I know that. But a lot of people don't think that way. There's a lot of older cats that's jealous of a brother like me; envious too. They won't let me know that, but I'm a person who can sense and have a feel to see a certain vibe a person gives me from their actions. For example, you can be on the phone with someone telling you one thing, but their actions show different: just something I've always been aware of. This goes back to high school and knowing who your true friends are. A brother like me never was the one to front to be with no clique or crew. I always kept to myself. That was the way I stayed out of drama. When I was younger that was different, because I had nothing to lose. But now it's like I have nothing to gain and too much to lose, because you can never stop learning.

It's Saturday and I'm with my road dog. I'm a single, young, black male, not even 21 yet, but thank God for fake IDs and modern technology. Right about now I need to have some fun. It has been a long time since I've been out and about. I've settled down since high school. God has blessed me with a nice job...a damn good job considering the fact that I was only 18 years old when I got it. God has been blessing me and it's all because of him that I've had so much success in my life. No words can describe how thankful I am for that. One day I sure hope that He blesses me with that one person that I can spend the rest of my life with. Maybe I'll meet her tonight...yeah right! In the club, there's nothing but freaks, but hey, you never know. You can meet that special person anywhere. You could meet that special person in the club, grocery store, or the mall. If it's meant to be, it's meant to be. Everything is everything. But me, I'm not the type of person who can approach a stranger. I just look at that special lady who catches my eye, then I smile, wave, or maybe even wink. But I could never get myself to approach that special one; probably a complex I had about getting dissed. Sometimes that's the worst feeling, and sometimes it might not matter depending on who you approach, but if I do approach a lady, I do come correct. None of that "Hey baby, what's up" shit. You have to have self-respect. Approach someone with the utmost respect. You will have a better conversation that way, and the lady will respect you more, depending on the woman, but I'm not looking for no one. Whatever happens just happens and I'll take it from there.

So, I'm going to sit back, chill, and have a nice time. It's kind of hard when the person who is driving is tipsy. Damn, what am I thinking? I need my butt whooped for being in this car. Forget it! If he swerves one more time, it's over. I'm going to have to say something. The person who is driving is a guy I'm associated with at work named Rick. He works first shift. He has just broken up and divorced his wife because she cheated on him, so right now he's not caring about anything. The guy in the passenger side is a cool cat named Jim. Real cool cat, just watch what you say and do around him. People are bound to know all your business when you get back to work. It's all good, but I know what type of level to keep it on with him, so it's cool. Whatever happens, nothing seems to bother him. No matter what it is. Money problems, female problems, and even problems at work, he never seems to break-most of the time anyway.

Sometimes I wish I had those traits or genes. But for me, Dre, everything somehow finds its way to getting to me. As the same goes, "pressure breaks pipes". I'm the easy-going, more laid-back type. I listen to rap but not that commercial shit. I like that real hardcore, got some meaning to it shit. The realest, illest type, even though I'm not that way. I like the creativeness of it too, but sometimes I like that laid-back shit. A little DeBarge, Stevie, Al Green, or Donny Hathaway; that soulful R&B, not that lick you up and down shit. But on the real, I been more into something with meaning behind it that I can relate to and feel. Some of those songs just talk about sex and lust. What about loving someone, caring about him or her, and sharing special moments? Something you can hold on to for years to pass, not just a nut. It's nothing behind that. I'm looking for the long haul, marriage even. If that right one comes along, maybe I will get married. Who knows if or when this will happen, but lately I've been playing it by if a female pursues me within a day or two; just sweating each chance she gets to see me; just talking about us going out or me coming over right offhand, then something is wrong if it's like that. Maybe she just likes me a lot, that could be true. But if you're not in a relationship with a person or you just met the person and she sweating you already, to me that draws up a red flag. That's not good in my book...I'm sorry. Asking questions that only married people ask each other, like where you been or just popping up out of the blue surprising you. That's when I draw the line, but enough about that.

I'm supposed to be telling you readers about my night out and if I found that special lady or not. Forgive me for that, it's just so little that happened this night out and so much that I gained from it, or so I thought. But you never know what you truly have until it's gone. We have all heard that before and it may have happened to you already. Love and loss. That key word LOVE has come a long way since before time and time again. Over and over you hear it. Does anyone really know what true love is? I must admit, as of now, I don't; I never been in a true relationship; long-term anyway. But this is my night out and anything can happen. I'm 6’2”, dark skinned, and a young attractive brotha. Something has got to give. Matter of fact, I'm the only dark-complexioned person in the car. Yellow brothers are played out anyway. I'm not a hater though. It's about where your mind level is at. A lot of people get caught up on looks and not the person for who they are. If I'm going to be with someone for the rest of my life, I want to be able to look at them every day without getting tired of them. So, it has to be some type of physical attraction. I'm not saying drop dead gorgeous, but at least an eight-piece. At least you want to be with someone you are proud and happy to be with, no matter what anyone has to say. As long as you are happy, that is what's important. I'm not conceited, but I deserve just as much as the next man. I'm a nice, attractive, self-respected, young, black male that wants something out of life. I just want somebody that respects herself and can handle her own responsibilities. Someone that doesn't always need anybody to be there by her side all of the time. Somebody that is understanding, intelligent, and strong-minded. They don't have to even have a fancy car, a big crib, or fly clothes. As long as she loves herself and is willing to work hard for what she wants, that's worth more than any fly car or house. If you work hard and put God first, everything will work out for the better. Be true to yourself and know what direction you want to go. Don't be a follower. Well, that about sums it up. Wait...I forgot, I don't want to deal with nobody's baby's daddy. I can make an exception for one child, but when you got two or three and I have none, that's a big responsibility. Then you have to deal with the baby's daddy. I don't need that headache too! Well, it's the 90s, so I know some nice young lady is going to have at least one child. Maybe not, but that's just the way things are nowadays. Born today and gone tomorrow.

Chapter 2 - Club Scene
(When We First Met)

It has been 40 minutes, and we finally hit Grand Rapid's city limits. After about 20 minutes of swerving, Jim and Rick trade spots. Rick was a little too tipsy, so Jim decided to take over driving. *Thank goodness*, I thought. *We would have never made it*. "Jim, good thing you took over, man...Rick was about to kill us," I said.

Rick just waved it off like it wasn't any big deal, like always, but Jim responded, "Aw, it was nothing. Rick just had too many gin and juices."

"Whatever," I said. "Gin and juice my ass – more like crack and Juice! He was swerving too damn much."

"Shut up!" Rick replied. "You all are just exaggerating. I hope it's some honeys in this club." Rick changed the subject.

"Man please, it's going to be the same played out hoes like usual," I said.

Jim replied, "Stop being so negative, Dre. It's not how many hoes are in the club, but which one you can take home."

Everyone laughs. "Whatever," I replied. "I don't get down like that. Not with shit like AIDS or Hepatitis B, C, D, 9, 10, or 20 out there."

"That's what they make condoms for," Jim replied.

"Those condoms are only 98% effective, so that don't mean jack. It can bust."

"There you go with that...your conscience gets to you too much."

"That's all good," I said. "Because your conscious could save your life. So be aware of shit like that. You probably been hittin' bitches raw, stupid ass.

“What you don't know won't hurt,” Jim replied.

“I know you got something for saying that bullshit!” I said. “I'm just trying to say that I'm not into that screwing stuff anymore. I want to settle down with the special lady who wants to spend the rest of her life with me. Not just sex...you can do that and nothing good comes out of it.”

“Yes it do,” Jim said. “A nice long nut!”

Everybody laughs. “See, that's why your girl don't trust you now. You don't take situations serious,” I added.

“Whatever,” Jim replied and laughed.

We finally pulled up to Club 54 in Grand Rapids, a place that is known to everybody who lives in small ass Muskegon. The club scene is looking kind of tight as we walk up to the door. Only 20 years old, I'm kind of nervous of the fake ID I'm about to use. I'm going to think positive thoughts instead of negative. I have a good vibe about tonight; I got to get in here.

"Dre, stand behind me so you can get through them little bit easier," Jim instructed.

"Alright, here goes nothing," I said. As I handed the bouncer my ID, I said a little prayer. Then boom, I was in.

Once inside, Jim says, "You were praying your ass off, wasn't you?"

"Without a doubt," I said. "And we're in here.

We were all walking around checking out the scene. Rick is already messed up, so he walks off into the crowd. "Alright man," Jim says to Rick. "Don't get lost."

Rick waves his hand at him and walks off. Lee, Jim, and myself walk straight up to the bar. As Jim tries to get the bartender's attention, I ask Jim to order my Hennessy on the rocks. Jim orders himself a rum and coke, and Lee orders a drink nobody has ever heard of. He is the kind of a person that doesn't give a shit.

Once we get our drinks, we start to go our separate ways.

“You know what time it is,” Jim says as we all nod our heads in acknowledgement. “See you at 2:00.”

I make my way around the club a couple of times and get approached by a couple of swollen women. They were cute, just a little too heavy.

“Hey cutie,” one says. “Are you here by yourself?”

“No,” I said.

Well, where is your wife.

“She should be around somewhere,” I try to play it off.

"She better hurry up and find you before we snatch you up."

I laugh a little bit. "I'll see you around."

"I bet you will." They then walk away. *Damn, that always happens to me*, I think. A big woman thinks because I'm skinny, I want her big ass. No offense, I like a woman with meat on her bones, but enough meat for me, not a tribe. Forgive me, but I'm just being real. As I make my way around for about the third time, I finally decide to just sit down. *I just don't see anything worth talking to*, I think to myself. They all look like tramps and gold diggers. I make eye contact a couple of times with some straight-up, ghetto-fabulous women. I had to look away quick. *It's time to move again*, I say to myself.

As I get up, I look to my left, then my right, and that's when I see her. She has a light complexion, she 5'

2'', classy...very classy. Her haircut is like Miss Greer off the Steve Harvey Show. She was it; the one. Now a brotha' like me is thinking, *"What are you waiting for?"*, but my legs wouldn't move. My game is kind of rusty. *What should I do? Damn, I hate when that happens.* Most of the time I would hesitate and end up saying nothing, just looking and drooling on myself. *Fuck it! The worst she can say is I got a man, or I'm not interested.* I just hate the feeling of getting rejected...in other words, dissed. *Alright Dre, let's do this.*

As I'm walking towards her, I see a couple of her friends with her. Now I'm getting kind of scared, hoping she doesn't diss me while all of her friends are around, knowing how a woman criticizes you up and down if your game is not up to par. I take a deep breath and swallow real hard, lick my lips, check my breath, and make sure I'm coming correct. "Excuse me, my name is Dre. How are you doing?"

"Fine," she replies.

"You're very attractive...what is your name?"

"Lannette. Hello Dre, nice to meet you," she says before I return the sentiment. She looks at my head first, then my shoes, then works her way back up to my teeth. As I'm looking at her, I take a moment thinking to myself, "*Damn she's a quarter piece fine as a dime piece!*" She was classy, none of that hoochie mama shit, with nice hips, lips, a pretty smile, and a hairstyle that fit her perfect; she was out cold. I mean, I was looking at her like I was sprung already just by looks alone. Now if she has a good head on her shoulders too, respect and love herself, it's on. "Well I was wondering if I could have five minutes of your time away from this area, like on the other end of the bar."

She looks at me again and smiles before replying, "Yeah okay,"

As I’m walking, I can see her friends smiling and looking at me out of the corner of my eye. That's a good sign, I hope. I turn around again to see if they're still looking. They are, so I play it off and wave at them. Walking to the other side of the bar, I'm thinking about what I want to talk about. I didn't even think I was going to get this far. *Damn Dre, just be yourself. Be honest and straight up with her.* I was concerned about my age and if I should tell her the truth. I don’t want her not to talk to me or give me her number. I want to make a good first impression. I'm thinking if I tell her my age, maybe she won't talk to me or give me her number. As I contemplate my next moves, her friend approaches me saying hello.

“I’m Shannel.”

“What's up,” I respond, motioning for them both to have a seat. Lannette smiles at me as Shannel looks at me real closely like she wants to eat me. She has some meat on her bones and she's very pretty. Lannette seems to glow as she looks at me. I was digging her like a grave.

"Where are you from?" I asked Lannette.

"Benton Harbor," she responds.

"Oh yeah, I know a couple of people from there where I live in Muskegon."

"You're from Muskegon?"

"Yes...the SKE, as people say. I like the different scenery and new faces."

"I know what you mean," she says, looking at my hand. "What's that in your hand?

"Just a piece of paper with your name on it. I'm hoping to put your phone number on it."

Her and her friend look at each other and smile. "Oh, that's nice. Was that your plan?" Lannette asks as she takes the paper from me and begins to write her number. I'm thinking to myself, *"It's Dre day once again."* I try to hide my smile, but I think Shannel caught me smiling a little.

"Well Dre, where's your lady at?" Shannel questions me.

"I don't have one of those," I reply.

"A good looking man like you?"

"You know how it is most of the time - women are not looking for much more than just a fling and I'm beyond that."

"There's nothing wrong with that," Shannel responds as Lannette hands me back the paper with her number and instructs me to not lose it.

I look at her and smile as I hand her my phone number, saying, "Don't you lose this."

She takes it and smiles back. “You were prepared.”

“When I saw you, I knew I had to be.

Shannel interjected, “You're just too much with all the right answers.”

“Let's just say that I'm at my best in clutch situations,” I say as they laugh. “When you’re a nervous young brotha’ like myself, you have no choice. You will either gain points or lose them.”

“Oh, I see,” Lannette responds, then goes into the one question I was trying to avoid all night. “So Dre, how old are you anyway?”

“I'm 21,” I lie, saying it slowly.

“I'm 22. Well, I'll be turning 22 in September, and since it's so close to the month I might as well claim it,” she says. “So, you're 21...it's nothing wrong with that. We are about to walk around and find the rest of our friends.”

"Okay, well, have fun and don't forget about me," I say.

"Don't worry, I'll keep your number in a safe place," she replies.

"Alright, be careful out there."

As they both smile and walk off, I say to myself, *Damn, I almost messed myself up*. But I'm good under pressure. I watch them walk away then see another dark chocolate fine honey walking my way. *Aw shit,* I say to myself. *Like Marvin Gaye said, what's going, on what's going on!* This woman is like figure eight status. She has a pretty smile and it's not often I get a lot of those. She looks at me like she's out for blood, saying hello in a sweet voice.

"What's up?" I respond.

"Is someone sitting here?"

"Not anymore."

She sits down real slow like she wants me to see every curve of her body. She introduces herself as Kim, then I tell her my name.

"It's nice to meet you," she says. So, Dre...why are you sitting alone?"

"I just am."

"Where's your woman or friends?"

"My friends are around somewhere. And my woman? I don't know the meaning," I reply.

"So, you don't have one?" Kim questions.

"You got it."

"Would you like to dance?"

"Sure," I say, hoping that Lannette won't see me. I should have turned Kim down. By the way she and her body smiled at me, I couldn't resist. As we walk to the dance floor, she grabs my hand. *Aw, here we go with this shit. She's already holding my hand*, I think. *I hope I'm not walking with a nutcase*. I try to pull away a little bit, but she is holding on for dear life. We get to the dance floor in time for a slow jam, which is cool, but she wants to dance all in the light. I move us back off in a darker spot, so now I'm a little bit more relaxed. As we dance, Kim tells me that she is from Lansing, and I share the same details, as well as how I work in a factory for a living. “Really? you don't look like a factory worker,” she says. “Anyway, it doesn't matter. I think you are a very handsome man and we need to get better acquainted.”

“Oh yeah, why is that?” I ask.

“Because once you get to know me I think you want to stay knowing me.”

"Oh yeah?" I knew what she was getting at. "What do you do?"

"Well, in a couple of weeks I will be a sheriff in Lansing Township," Kim replies.

"Interesting. So how old are you?"

"I'm 29. Does it matter?"

"You tight," I say, but I'm thinking to myself, *Damn!* When she asks, I tell her the fake age that I've been using all night, before she goes into the topic of kids. "I love kids, but I don't think I could handle it or take care of any right now. That's a big responsibility."

"Try taking care of five," Kim replies.

"Damn!" I thought I said it in my mind, but I apparently said it aloud.

"What did you say, Dre?"

"Oh nothing." I respond. That isn't a family—she already got a miniature hoop squad. "You do not look like you have five kids," I said to break my awkward silence.

"Why do you say that, Dre?"

"Because your body doesn't show it. I just don't see how you do it all by yourself."

"It's not easy," she replies. "But you have to have a lot of patience and firmness."

"I guess so," I say, and I laugh a little bit. When the song ends, we start walking back to where we were sitting, and she grabs my hand again. I'm looking around being cautious, as she tells me how much she enjoyed dancing with me. She hands me a piece of paper with her number on it and she says, "Use it sometimes."

"Sure thing," I say, as I notice that she kind of lingers and waits, I guess to see if I will give her my number. *No chance!*

"Bye Dre," she says and finally walks off.

I still couldn't believe she has five kids. *Oh well, I'm not going to be able to do it, baby*. I sit and chill solo for a minute, until Lee and Jim approach me. Jim immediately starts asking about Kim, that is until I mention the five kids. "Damn!" says both Lee and Jim together, ending all conversation about Kim.

"Where is Rick at?" I ask.

"I don't know," Jim replies. "I seen him once, then I didn't see him no more. He probably in the car passed out."

It was about that time to go. "Let's hit it. Let's see if we can catch some strays," Jim says.

"Here you go with that," I say, as we began heading toward the front door. I saw her again...Lannette. She was smiling and looking straight at me. I gave her a smile right back.

"Damn," Lee says. "Who is that, Dre?"

"Just a little something something. You know me," I say with a grin.

"Look at you...always on some sneaky shit," Jim adds.

"I'm not sneaky. She's not even from around here. She is from Benton Harbor. She's tight too."

"Boy you better handle it before I do."

"Too late nigga, it's already handled, homie" I respond. "She's the one.

As we make our way through the doors, its mass hysteria outside. Cars are everywhere, crowds of people, and it's off the knob. There are too many black folks to recognize anybody right now, as we keep an eye out looking for Rick. You know how they say we all look alike anyway? But I do see a familiar face again.

"Are you following me?" Lannette asked

"No, are you following me" I respond, noticing she is holding on to Shannel's shirt.

Noticing me watching, Lannette says, "I don't want to get lost."

"Don't worry, I'll protect you out here; you straight with me."

"Well aren't you the gentleman. Well, we are about to go. We're just looking for our other friend then we're out of here."

"Alright Lannette...don't forget about me," I say.

When she responds with a smile, I feel like a child on Christmas morning.

I walk around a little more until I see Jim and Lee talking to a couple of women. "Let's go!" I yell.

"Hold up," Jim says. "You got yours, now I'm getting mine."

I laugh at him as they get their numbers then head toward me. "You get the digits?"

"Hell yeah! Them tricks from Africa," Jim says.

"Aw shit," I say. "You're fuckin' with them crazy ass butt naked women. They gonna fuck around and put a root on y'all asses."

"That's a Haiti bitch," Jim says.

"They are all the same," I respond. We all laugh walking up to the car. We see throw up by the door. And there Rick is, passed out in the car.

"Well Jim, looks like you will be driving again," Lee says.

"One of those weekends," Jim replies.

And what a great weekend. As we drive out of the parking lot, I have Lannette on my mind.

Chapter 3

(The Following Week Phone Conversation)

It's just another manic Monday, and I have to go to work in less than an hour. It just hit lunchtime and I'm just now getting ready. I hate Mondays and I hate going to this damn factory all the damn time. Three years out of high school and it's the same old bullshit. Damn, I don't feel like going in today. I should take a vacation day. Fuck it, I'll take one Friday so I will have a longer weekend. That's the only time I have a life, being on second shift. As the phone rang, I wondered who could this be, hoping it's Lannette. Would she call this soon? I pick up the phone on the second ring. I heard a sweet hello on the other end. "Is Dre home?"

Right away I knew it was her. She has a voice that you will never forget. "Speaking," I say eagerly.

"How are you doing?"

"Real good, now that I'm talking to you," I respond.

I told her although I was getting ready for work, I had time to speak to her. "What shift do you work?"

"I work mornings most of the time, but it varies," Lannette says.

"You like working like that I ask?"

"It depends on if my mother works the same time as I do, because I have to make sure she can babysit for me."

Damn, she's got a baby daddy. "So how many kids you have?"

"Just one."

"What a relief," I say out loud, not intending to.

"What you say, Dre?"

"Oh nothing. That's good. As long as you didn't say three, four, or five, cause...damn!"

Lanette laughs in a sweet voice then says, "Is this a problem?"

"No, not at all-no problem at all. You could have eight kids and it still wouldn't matter."

"Aw, aren't you sweet."

We only talked for a few more minutes, with me telling her that I'd call her during my break at 6:30 pm, which she said was perfect. As she tried to end the call, I interrupted, "Wait, I have a couple more minutes to talk?"

"I'm sorry Dre, I had Shannel call from her job because I don't have long distance calling on my phone."

"No problem...no problem at all."

"I'll talk to you on your break, Dre," Lannette says.

"Yeah I'll be looking forward to it," I reply before we end the call. I hung up the phone grinning away, feeling real good. Now I can go to work happy today. Yes, she called first and usually I'm the first one to call a female. She must really dig a brotha'. *It's all goo*d, I think to myself as I put my socks and shoes on. I grab my coat, and hit the door. Soon as I get in the car, I bump D'Angelo. I'm in a good mood, so I'll listen to some R&B today. Usually I'm straight hip-hop going into work. Lannette called and I'm just overwhelmed with happiness. It's like love at first sight for me. She's a winner all the way; I can go on and on.

As I enter the factory parking lot, I feel good. I am ready to clock in and get these eight hours over with or at least four-and-a-half. My break isn't until 6:30 but as soon as 6:30 hits, I'm calling Lannette. I'll eat later...damn some food!

As soon as I make it to my work area, I can see Jim ready to tell my business. “Hey playa, playa!”

“Jim, you can't hold water.”

“What Dre? All I said was hey playa playa.”

“Whatever Jim!” Another person I work with, a lady named Judy, throws her nose up quick, wondering what he's talking about. Then there is Nick the comedian on the line; he's ready to take any little thing and make it a big joke. And we have Rochelle the college student who works during the summer. And Pamela who likes to add her two cents. I just got to the line and Jim already starting something. All the first shift is still here and he just jabbering away on what we did Saturday.

“So, what happened Dre?” is everyone’s question.

“Nothing.” I respond. “I just had a good time. that's all.”

"That isn't all," Jim says boisterously. "Tell them about the two hotties you were digging on."

"It was only one nice young lady, Jim, not two."

"What about that one with five kids, Dre?"

Right away, everyone looked at me. "Please...hell no," I say quickly. "You got a big mouth, man. I'm not going anywhere else with your ass because you talk too much. Everyone from first shift is gonna leave calling me Daddy."

Everyone continues laughing and cracking funny jokes. "That's alright," I finally say. "Y'all will see her sooner or later at the picnic. Don't worry about it until then. Now get out of my face, bastards," I say jokingly.

Everyone continues laughing but they still want to know who's the special lady I met. And you guessed it, Jim tells it all. He can't hold anything back. "I know she's from Benton Harbor."

"Damn Jim, can you be quiet for two seconds? It's not even 2:30 yet!"

Jim goes on with the show like he doesn't hear me. "She's a tight little redbone. Dre was damn near creaming himself talking' about her on the way home.

Everyone laughs for the next 20 seconds as I decide to turn the jokes on him. "Please Jim, you just mad you met some bush bitch from Africa." Everybody busts out laughing again, this time even harder.

"Alright Dre, I'm going to leave you alone."

"No Jim, keep on with your blabbering, 'cause I can go on and on about them bush bitches."

Everybody laughs again, and but it finally starts to die down. Now I can finally think of some things to talk about when I call Lannette. We joke around a bit more while we work, and next thing I know it is 6:30. I head straight to the pay phone. As I head to the phone, I get butterflies in my stomach hoping that it's free. There are only two phones in the shop; the one by the front door hallway is the best because you can hear well, and it happens to be available. The other one in the shop you, can't hear on it at all because of people getting paged in the shop over the loudspeaker. I make sure I have enough change. I don't care if it cost $20 to call, I'm calling. I dial the number. "That will be $.50 please for the first three minutes," the operator announces.

I put the money in anxiously. *Hurry, hurry,* I say to myself. I only have 20 minutes. The call goes through, and it rings and rings, until I finally hear her say hello.

"Hello, what's up with you, Lannette?"

"Hey Dre, I was waiting for your call."

"Yeah right," I say jokingly.

"Seriously, Dre."

I notice her breathing. "Why are you breathing so hard?"

"I was washing, so I was running to get to the phone to catch your call," she says.

"So, what's the deal with seeing you again?"

"You don't really want to see me again, do you Dre?" Lannette replies.

"Does Michael Jordan slam dunk?" I ask back. "You better believe I want to see you again." We discuss what works best for our schedules, and I inform her how my weekends work best. "I was thinking about you coming to my company picnic with me if you aren't busy? It's Saturday and Sunday. We could do either day."

"Let me check with my mother or maybe I can get my son's father to watch him"

“If you want, you can bring him along,” I offer.

“No, it'll be alright this time, Dre. Maybe next time once we get to know each other more,” Lannette suggests.

“That's cool, I understand. That’s the respectful thing for you to do-not just having any Tom, Dick, or Joe around your child. I understand completely. What about you though?”

“I'll check into it and let you know if I'm able to go.”

“That's cool with me,’ I say.

“Alright Dre, it was nice talking to you again.”

“Maybe I'll give you a call when I get home, if you're not busy?”

She agreed that would be fine, so we said our goodbyes and I hung up the phone feeling good. Good conversation is a key factor when you want to get to know someone, especially long distance. It's also a disadvantage because you don't know what the person's expression is. I guess that's something I'm going to have to adapt to. As I walked back to my work area, I'm realize I'm five minutes late from break. Soon as I reach the line, I hear Jim's mouth.

"Hey, what did you do, have phone sex?"

Everybody on the line laughs. "Don't get jealous, Jim. I'm sure your bush woman will call you from Zimbabwe."

"Alright, alright...I'm going to leave it alone, Dre," Jim says.

"Alright then 'cause I can crack all night," I say.

"I think it's sweet that Dre met him someone," Judy adds. Now Judy is a nice sweet older lady. She's about 46 but looks like she's 30. She's real sweet and understanding but can be sneaky and a little nosy. She seems to be good people though.

"They're just jealous of me, that's all." I say to her.

"That's right, Dre," Judy says back

"Be careful though, Dre," Nick adds his two cents. "Don't let the beauty fool you." Now Nick is an older cat who been through it all. Slaved some of the best woman but he's married now. He has two kids to bring up in this world, so he had to do what was best for him. He's real self-maintained and focused; someone you can go to for advice.

"I hear you, Nick," I say.

Everybody's breaks rotate for the second go around and time flies by before it's 10 and time to get the hell out of dodge. I usually go work out after work, but I'm going home to call Lannette.

"You not going to the gym tonight," Nick asks as we head out of work.

"Not tonight Nick. I got business to take care of."

"Alright Dre, you gonna blow up!"

"One night won't hurt me."

"Alright Dre, see you tomorrow." Nick says as we clock out. Now I'm ready for the E-way; 15 minutes and I'm home; tonight I make it in 10 minutes. I rush in the house, throw my clothes off, shower, get in my boxers, and grab the phone. But I forget one thing. I have a block on my phone. *Shit!* I jump into whatever is closest. I run out of the door in some tight jogging pants, no shirt, and my mother's shoes that were by the door with the back of my feet over the heel. *Damn, what am I thinking*. That's the point, I wasn't. I just had a lot on my mind.

I finally make it to the store around the corner, but I only have $2 in change in the car. This will have to do. I dial the number, but the call is $1.90. Damn! So, now I'm driving from pay phone to pay phone trying to find one that doesn't charge that much. I might as well drive to where she's at. It's 11:30 already before I finally pull up to a gas station and dial the number. The operator announces, "That will be $.50 please." *Yes*! "Hello Lannette," I say when she answers.

"What's up, Dre?"

"You sound tired. Were you sleeping?" I ask her.

"No, just sitting here thinking," she says.

"Are you thinking about me?"

"Well, of course, Dre."

"What are you thinking about?"

"Seeing you again."

"I want to see you too. I wish I could see you now," I say before I decide to ask her about her son. His name is Demond Lamont McDaniel.

"Where's his father?" I ask.

"Somewhere around here. He comes around every now and then."

"He's crazy for that, Lannette."

"Why do you say that, Dre?"

"Because he's a fool to not want to take care of something he brought into this world and that carries the same blood as he does. And definitely a fool for not wanting to be with the beautiful woman that gave birth to his son."

"That's nice, Dre. I can tell you're a sweet person," Lannette says.

"That's just how my mother and father raised me," I respond.

"Yeah? They raised a dime piece."

"What you know about a dime piece?" I ask in surprise.

"That's what you are, Dre...a dime piece."

"Well, if I'm a dime piece, I'm looking at a quarter piece. I'm not going to lie," I continue. "When I first saw you, I had to say something. It was meant for me to say something, but I thought you would turn me away."

"Dre, I couldn't possibly do that to you because you're too cute."

"Thanks, that's nice to hear. But you were the one shining that night."

"Dre, you always find some way to make the nicest compliments."

"Well you have so many nice features. You can't help but to say nice things."

"There you go again," Lannette says.

"Alright, I hear you, but I can't help it. You're just a beautiful lady and I'm glad we met."

"Me too, Dre."

As we continued talking, she told me that it had been a while since she last saw her son's father. "Alright but don't be playing with my emotions now," I jokingly said, but I was serious inside.

"No don't worry about him," she replies.

"So, will I see you soon, Lannette?

"I'll give you a call before next week and let you know when I go back and visit my friend in Grand Rapids."

"That's cool." The operator interrupts with "$0.85 please." I hurry up and put the money in so I can talk a little longer. "So, you going to get a hold of me right?"

"Yes, I will, Dre."

"Alright...don't have me coming up there looking for you."

"That won't be necessary. I'll make sure of that."

"Stay sweet, alright," I say.

"I will."

It was hard for me to hang up because it was so much more that I wanted to talk about. Hopefully, she can come to the picnic with me. That will give us some time and maybe I will just flat out tell her how old I am. What do I have to lose? I just want to be straight up and honest because I really think she is the one. As I'm driving home, she's all I can think about. It always seems that way. I meet a nice lady that is not in the same city as me. That's the only thing that kind of concerns me. A lot of people say that long-distance relationships don't work. I have a good laugh about her. If it's just meant, it's meant. Everything is everything.

Chapter 4

(Weekend to Remember)

Friday, one day before the picnic...it's about 7:30 a.m. I always get up early so I can handle a little business. For one thing, I need a nice haircut. These naps on my head got to go. My barber always bullshits on this day. I got up early so I can make sure I'm first in his chair because he's the type that wants to take his time to come to work. He'll tell you he'll be there at 9 a.m. and won't make it in until 12 p.m. That's a typical nigga for you. I haven't heard from Lannette in about a week and I really didn’t want to bug her or nothing. So, I figure if she wants to go to the picnic or see me, she will call; well, I hope she does. If she doesn't call me by the time I'm finished with my haircut, I'm going to call her.

As I walk out the door, the phone rings. It's probably a bill collector, I think, but I check anyway. "Out of Area" is what the caller ID reads. When I answer, I'm excited to hear Lannette's voice on the other end.

"What are you doing this weekend, Dre?" she asks me.

"Trying to be wherever you are, Lannette," I reply.

"Well, I'll be in Grand Rapids this weekend. Are you coming to see me?

"No question...you don't have to say another word."

As Lannette gave me Tami's phone number so I'd be able to reach her once I got to Grand Rapids, I was happy and excited. "Will you be able to go to the picnic?"

"I don't see why not."

"Okay then, then I'll see you tomorrow," I say.

"Looking forward to it," Lannette responds.

"Me too."

We hang up the phone and now I'm really excited. I'm out the door and ready for my haircut. I get to the barbershop and there's nobody there, which is good because service is on a first-come, first-serve basis, so I'm first today. I can go to work happy for a change as long as my barber comes on time. Speaking of him, he pops up with a big smile on his face.

"About time," I say to him jokingly. "You must be sick or got an illness or something. This is the first time in a long time you ever came this early. You need to do it more often."

"Whatever," he says with a grin on his face. "I'm here, that's all that matters."

"Yeah, well let's do this so I can get these naps taken care of."

"Why do you seem in a rush?" my barber questions me.

"I got to go see somebody tomorrow, so I have to look my best," I reply.

"You still going to be hit with or without a haircut!"

"I see you trying to get your crack on early today."

"The truth is the truth," he says with a big smile.

"Please...your pants so tight, you can see the face of Abraham Lincoln on that penny in your pocket," I crack, and he then laughs.

"Alright Dre, I'm through cracking with you," my barber says as we look at one another waiting for the jokes to start back up. “You crazy, I'm through messing with you, Dre.”

As he finishes my hair, people start rolling in. That's when all the gossip starts. Niggas be talking worse than women. I'm glad I avoided this today. I give my barber the money and say thanks.

“See you next week.”

“Alright Dre, let me know how things go with the young lady you met.”

I walk out the shop anticipating getting to work and getting it over with. I make it to work after taking care of everything I needed to on this beautiful sunny day. It's hard for me to go in and do these eight hours, but what the hell; I'm in a good mood and can't wait until tomorrow.

As I get to the line and start working, I keep looking at the clock, which is making the day long. I get my Walkman to take my mind off the clock and time starts cutting away. There wasn't really much joking during break today. Everybody was ready to go, and Fridays always last long because it's the last day of the week. It's good we don't have to work tomorrow because of the picnic. After the second round of breaks, and getting through the shift, everyone shouted out their goodbyes, but not before asking me about who I was bringing to the picnic with me.

"We will see," I simply said with a grin.

Saturday is finally here. I woke up early for this day. I showered, dressed, and packed my things because I plan on getting a room, so if she wants to go somewhere to chill, she can. After making sure I haven't forgotten anything, I put my things in the car, then check the oil and fluids to make sure the Delta is running tight. I hope she's not a car person. You know the kind of woman that wants you to have a certain type of car in order to like you. My car is alright for an older model, but it is clean, like me. I stay clean, and you can tell a lot about a person that way. If they keep their car clean, the more it is that they keep themselves that way. If not, you know the deal on that.

After I tell my mother and father that I'll be gone for the weekend, the questions begin. "Where are you going, Dre? Who are you going to see?" my mother asks.

"There is somebody, ma...you'll see in due time."

"Alright boy, don't be bringing no babies back here."

My father had something to say too. "What you doing, Dre...moving? Because it looks like you packed a lot of clothes."

"Pops, I'll be gone through Sunday."

"Oh...okay then," pops said as if it wasn't a big deal.

Walking to my car after saying my goodbyes, I'm too excited to get out of Muskegon. It's about a 45-minute drive from Muskegon to Grand Rapids, but today I will probably make it in 25 minutes. I make sure everything is secure, so now I'm ready to roll and hit the E-way. I pop some Jay-Z in the CD player; "It's Alright" is playing. *Yeah, everything will be alright*, I say to myself. As I roll along, I make it to Grand Rapids in about 30 minutes exactly. I'm feeling real good right about now. I'm anxious to see that beautiful face again.

I make it to a pay phone and dial the number Lannette gave me to her friend Tami's apartment. Someone picks up and says hello. I ask for Lannette, and she's on the phone immediately.

"Hey, Dre?"

"Yeah, this is I."

"You made it," she says, then letting me know that she's still not dressed yet. "Where are you?"

"I'm at a gas station on 28th Street."

"Okay, I'll have Tami give you directions." Once Tami got back on the phone and gave me my directions on getting there, I start driving through Grand Rapids trying to find a nice room to stay at. I don't want just any old room. I don't want her to get the wrong idea. So, I just decide to go to the Holiday Inn, one of the most expensive hotels. Oh well, it's only one night. It might not be that much. I go up to the front desk and the only thing available is a king-size room only for $89 a night. Damn for one night to sleep? I was wondering if steak and eggs got served with it cause damn that is a lot of money! But I went ahead with it. For that much, I better spend the majority of my time in the room.

I try to keep my mind occupied on the conversation I will have with Lannette and not on how much money I paid for the room. I'm not hurting or nothing, but these are baller prices. But I had to think for a minute...for Lannette I would have paid $200 per night. The way she carries herself, I never thought about the price of the room again. With her, money was no object. She was that type of lady. As I continued thinking on what kind of conversation to spark, I decided I would just ask the Lord to help me out on this one. I haven't been out with no one in a while, and I mean a while. I pull up to the apartments with butterflies in my stomach; I'm anxious to see her. I get out the car, walk up to the door with my usual pimp walk, trying not to pimp too hard though. I rang the doorbell and take a deep breath. Lannette's friend Tami answers the door with a big smile on her face. “Hey you must be Dre,”she says looking at me from head to toe. “It's a pleasure to meet you.”

“Same here,” I say.

“Lannette has to finish getting ready but she'll be right out,” Tami adds as she motions me to come inside. That’s when I see Shannel, who also greets me.

“So, where are you two lovebirds going?” Shannel asks. I tell both ladies of my plans, and they make me feel even better about my date with Lannette. “Dre, that’s nice. I think you and Lannette will hit it off pretty well.”

“Do you really think so?” I ask for confirmation, in which both ladies nod their heads. “Perfect,” I say, trying my hardest to hide my smile.

“Yeah Dre, from what Lannette told me, you seem like the perfect gentleman...cool and laid-back. That's the kind of man I look for.”

“Well, maybe if you don't look for it, it will come to you,” I suggest.

“That's true, that's true,” Shannel replies.

“So, you got a brain with those good looks too,” Tami states.

“It's just common sense, that's all,” I say. That’s when I hear Lannette’s sweet voice announcing that she is ready. Damn, this girl is a gold piece. All she has on is a t-shirt and jeans, and she still looks outstanding.

“Give me a hug,” Lannette orders of me, and I don't hesitate to give her that hug. “Oh, you give nice warm hugs. Dre, you’re so tall though; it's like I will never stop reaching for you.”

“I don't mind bending down for you. I like your height,” I respond. “But that's not all I like either.”

Everyone in the room looks at each other and Lannette begins to blush. “Isn't he just too much, y'all? she says to her friends. “Were they out here blowing your head up, Dre?”

“No, not too much. They're alright with me. They're real cool and down-to-earth.”

We continue chatting and giggling for a few about another minute before Lannette tells them we’re about to leave.

“Yeah, y'all save all that energy for later,” Shannel jokes and giggles.

“Alright, we are out of here,” I interject.

"Wait a minute, let me take a look at you two together. You two make a great couple," Shannel continues as Tami nods in agreement. "Y'all have fun."

"See you later," I reply before we head out to the car. I make sure I open the door for her. I want to start our date off on a good note.

"Thanks, Dre."

"It's my pleasure."

"So, where are we going?" Lannette inquires.

"Probably to a matinee, go get something to eat, and then to the mall. That way, I feel we can talk a bit to get to know each other."

"I'm cool with that."

Then I remember that I better tell her about the hotel room, in which she responds in curiosity, "Why did you do that?"

"Well, I figured if we both were going to be up here and you wanted to relax or something, we can go there to kick back for a while," I explain.

"Oh, I see. Well, I'm cool with that, that's all good," she says in a more mellow tone.

As I drive, she compliments me on my ride. "It's nice and roomy."

"It's alright now. I put some money into it though. It didn't look like this when I first got it."

"Well, I like the rims and it has a pretty color to it," she adds.

"Thank you. That's a nice thing to say," I reply. "You have a pretty color, pretty face, and a pretty smile."

"Dre, you always saying something sweet."

"Because you know it's the truth. Everything about you is precisely right."

Lannette blushes and shakes her head, then says thanks. As we drive around Grand Rapids, we talk about our likes and dislikes, as well as a little bit about our pasts. I try to be more humorous than anything to try to keep her laughing. I want this to be more on a friendship level at first, but as we got to talking, we were letting each other in on some things you wouldn't tell your best friend. It's like we were on the same level. She couldn't believe the fact that I was single with no kids. I think that was what attracted her the most. We were both being upfront and honest with each other through our conversation, except the part about my age. I'm questioning myself the whole time on should I tell her the truth. We were having such a good time laughing one minute and serious the next on certain topics, I didn't want to spoil the moment, so I just forgot about it.

We also talked about how many people we had been with sexually. On this topic, I wasn't afraid to speak because it hasn't been many for me. When I told her there had only been a couple, she looked at me in disbelief. I explained to her the fact that I used to be a little overweight and how I was shy, so that made me less confident in approaching woman. She believed me. Lannette was understanding and interested in what I had to say, and I noticed that. I never met a lady like her or conversed with anyone for so long as I was with her. The conversation between us was nonstop and it never got quiet between us. I had the music playing but it had been turned down since we got in the car. We make to the movies and decide on Doctor Dolittle, but once we sit down we still continue conversing and just enjoying each other's company. Five minutes into the movie, we decide to just leave. Neither of us were really feeling the movie anyway, and our conversation continued to deepen. We went and sat on some benches outside the theater. I just stared at her and fell in love with her from that moment. I couldn't believe I found someone who was so understanding and just listens to me. We both were into each other deeply, and we both knew it. I finally asked her about the topic that it seemed she was dodging all day- about her baby's daddy. She said she hardly saw him, but that was kind of hard for me to believe. I took her word for it though. We were both being upfront and honest the whole time, so I'm thinking why would she lie now.

By this point we told one another what we like best about each other. I told her I like everything, even the fact that she has a child. I told her I would like to take my hat off to her for supporting both herself and her child and not receiving any help from her baby's daddy.

"In the long run, it will be his loss for not being there," I say, and Lannette smiles graciously and looks into my eyes deeply. She tells me again that I'm a sweet person. "I'm thankful and appreciative for everything that has happened since we met," I add.

"I feel the same way, Dre."

We had sat and talked for so long, the movie had let out and we hardly noticed the people that were coming out. We just laughed about the situation and began our way out to leave as well.

When we make our way back to her friend's apartment, no one is home and she doesn't have a key. I ask her does she want to spend the night with me since we're leaving out in the morning anyway for the company picnic at the amusement park.

"Are you sure, Dre?"

"Yes, I would like you to. And this will give us more time with each other," I reply. "The whole day have been lovely, and I don't want it to end."

Lannette smiles and agrees to spend the night with me. As we head back to the hotel, we agree that we'll stop back by the apartment for her to change in the morning before we head to the amusement park. When we get to the room, we are both ready for a nice shower and the bed. I showered first and she showered after me. As she prepared herself, all sorts of things are going through my head, including the sleeping arrangements. Out of the respect of the first night being together, I decide to just sleep on the couch. I grab a couple of pillows off the bed and the cover, then try to make myself comfortable the best way possible. The couch was kind of short, and my tall, skinny ass was covering it like gravy on mashed potatoes; arms over one way, legs over another. Lannette finally comes out of the bathroom smelling good and looking good enough to eat. *Damn, she is one fine Coppertone,* I say to myself. She looks at me with a smile. "What are you doing on the couch?"

"I want you to be comfortable, so I decided to just give you some space," I answer.

"If you say so, Dre." She reaches for the phone to call her friend and let her know where she is. I can hear laughter coming through from the other end of phone, and Lannette laughs along.

"What did they say?" I ask once they hang up.

"You know how they are always full of jokes," she says, then changes the subject. "Now Dre, are you sure you are okay over there on the couch?"

"Yeah, I'm fine."

"Well goodnight," she says, and I say goodnight back as she turns off the light. All I can think about is being in that bed next to her but I'm afraid I couldn't control myself if I was. She already smells good enough to eat from over here on the couch. If I was directly next to her, I probably wouldn't know how to act. It's been a while since I've been this close to another woman. *Man, I got to do what I got to do*, I say to myself. *I must keep my composure*.

"Nette," I say the nickname I came up with for her in a low tone. "You sleep?"

"Not yet Dre. What's wrong?"

"I was wondering could I..."

"You want to get in the bed?" She already knew what I was about to ask. "Come on over. Why didn't you just get in the bed anyway?" she says as I get up from the couch to head to the bed.

"Well, I don't want you to get the wrong idea about me and I respect you a lot. I didn't want you to lose the respect you have for me."

"You're so sweet. I knew you were special," she says, then reaches over to kiss me on the lips. Her lips are so soft, and I didn't mind it at all. I tell her thank you, then she smiles and says, "You don't snore, do you?"

"I don't think so, but if I do, just put the pillow over my head."

That makes her laugh. "I'll be all right, Dre."

"What's that perfume you have on?" I ask.

"You like it?"

"Hell yeah! You smell irresistible, woman."

Lannette blushes and laughs before reaching over to give me another kiss.

"Okay Lanette, you can't keep giving me them kisses like that and expect me to stay on my side of the bed." I'm joking but I'm serious too. She laughs again then tells me goodnight, but then we both meet each other halfway once more and give each other a nice polite and gracious kiss. I love every bit of it. She turns the light back out and then we are both sleeping like babies. The next morning, we get up, get our things together, I get dressed, and then we take her to her friend's place to get dressed too so we can prepare to continue this fun wonderful weekend. As I sit outside and wait for her to get ready and come back out, I hate to think it's all going to be over after this Sunday. But I'm making the best out of every minute we spend together. As Lannette tries to leave, Shannel and Tami are following her out trying to get her to tell them what happened last night, but Lannette just laughs them off. "Shannel, what time should I be back before we need to leave heading back?"

"Let's say 7 pm."

It was already 11 a.m., so we don't waste any time starting out on our quest to the amusement park. We make it back to Muskegon in about 30 minutes. Our first stop is to my house so I can introduce Lannette to my mother and father. Once we go in, Lanette seems pretty cool. I knew my mother and father would be surprised, because this is the first time I ever introduced any young lady that I met to them. I've never been in a relationship before. I never found a nice young lady that I could call my girlfriend. Lannette is the first and I hope it works out and she'll stay my only girlfriend. Only time will reveal.

We took a seat in the living room, and I shouted out to let my parents know I was there. When my mother came out of her room, she looked very surprised.

“Hello, Mrs. Powers, I’m Lannette”

“Hi honey,” my mother responds, still in disbelief of this pretty young lady sitting in her living room. “Dre, she's very pretty and has such a pretty smile. So where are you two going today? The church I hope?”

Lannette and I look at each other. “No, mama, remember...today is my company picnic so we're going to the amusement park.”

“Oh, I see. You two have a nice time,” my mother joked as she acted as if she were jealous to not be going. After a few questions for Lannette, including where she was from, my mother says," "The home of Sinbad!" in reference to the comedian. We all laugh, as my mother adds, "That's alright with me honey."

My father finally comes from the room on his way to church. I introduce them before he makes his way out the door. After that brief exchange, Lannette looks at me like she's a little concerned, not sure what to make of that meeting, but I reassure her that my dad is just laid back and not full of much emotion. "Yeah baby, he's just a little late for church," my mom adds to further reassure her. It was a pleasure meeting you, honey. I hope to see you again."

"Same here, Mrs. Powers."

Once we leave my parents, we head to the amusement park. We're both ready to have some fun and make the best of the rest of the time we have together today. We get there and notice immediately how hot it is. The first thing we do is get a couple of Icee's, then we walk around a bit to sightsee. I finally decide to try to win her a couple of stuffed animals. I wasn't going to quit until I did. I decide to go over to the weight guessing game, which I thought would be easy, and it was. It's pretty difficult for someone to guess my weight because people always forget to add in my height. The girl at the game couldn't guess my weight, so I was expecting a great big stuffed animal. Instead, she hands us a small furry troll. We laugh at that.

We then go on a ride called the Water Log. This gives us a little time to get close. I love every bit of it too. It kept going through my mind how I knew after this weekend I would probably be working the upcoming weekends like crazy. If there was anything I wanted to say to her, I'd better say it now. You couldn't make another one of her. I know that patience is a big factor when getting to know someone like her, but with Lannette it seems as if I knew her all my life. As we get a little wet on the water ride, we decide to get on The Swinger to dry off. As we are leaving that ride, I see a girl that I used to talk to. I was hoping that she wouldn't try to show her ass or anything. As we walk by her and one of her friends, I speak. She speaks back with a sour look on her face, which causes Lannette to look at me and ask if everything is alright. I tell her everything is cool. Inside, I'm trying to keep my composure on point. It was getting hotter, especially after that little run-in, so we decide to catch the shade and chat a little while. In my mind, I'm thinking I'll go ahead and be honest with her, laying everything out on the table about my age. I was quiet for a minute, but then Lannette finally breaks the silence to ask me if I'm alright. I tell her I was fine and asked her the same, trying to play it all off.

"I like you, Dre, and I know we just met and I know that we shouldn't rush anything, but I feel very at ease when I'm with you or talking to you, and I feel that if there's anything you want to talk to me about or say, don't be afraid to."

I was looking her directly in her eyes, when she suddenly asked, "You have a girlfriend, don't you, Dre?" She was looking disappointed.

"No!," I respond quickly. "It's my age." I immediately put my head down in shame. She grabs my hand and puts her other hand under my chin to lift my head up.

"Is that it, Dre?"

I shook my head yes. "I'm 20," I say in a low tone.

Lannette looks me straight in the eyes, as I'm thinking to myself that this is the end. But she leans over and kisses me. My eyes widen and my heart pumps faster. “Dre, you are a real gentleman. You didn't have to let me know that if you didn't want. I'm 100 miles away from you, and you could have kept that to yourself and I wouldn't have known anything.”

“So, you're not mad Lannette?”

“No...far from it. It just lets me know that you're serious about this and you have a good conscious.”

At that moment it was like a Kodak picture moment. Her and I were looking at each other. Love was in the air. We both lean in and meet each other with a nice kiss.

“Anything else Dre?”

“No, that's it,” I say, but then I have a question. “If I would have told you my real age that night I met you, would you have given me your number?”

“To be honest,” she says as she thinks for a moment. “Probably not.”

“Really?”

“Yeah, because I wouldn't have ever thought you were this mature. By the way, how did you get in the club that night?”

“Fake ID and a lot of praying!”

We both laughed and everything felt alright. Everything must have been meant to happen like this, I think to myself as I look directly into her eyes and we kiss. It will only get better. We get up and decide to try to win one more stuffed animal before calling it a day. As we walk, we run into Judy from work. She notices us right away, and I think, *"Oh, here comes trouble."* Judy's daughter Gina is with her, and so is Gina's little boy; both mother and daughter are smiling ear to ear.

"Dre, who is this pretty young lady?"

"Judy, meet Lannette; Lannette meet my coworker Judy."

"Nice to meet you," Julie replies first

"Same here," Lannette replies.

After a little bit of chitchat, and me telling Judy that we were going to be leaving once I won another stuffed animal, Judy looks at the stuffed animal that Lannette already had, and says, "That's cute!"

After saying our goodbyes, with Judy smiling and throwing up a "thumbs up" to me, we head to the water gun game where you aim at the clown's mouth. We were the only ones playing, so it was a win-win situation. I won the game and gave Lannette the stuffed animal of her choice, then we were ready to make our way back to Grand Rapids. On our way out, we spot Ronald, who is also from Benton Harbor.

"Are you leaving, Dre?"

"Yeah man, we had fun and it has to end somewhere. By the way, my bad, this is Lannette."

"Oh, I know, Dre." Ronald nods at her while Lannette looks like she's frustrated.

After asking me about the tournament at the gym, Ronald ends the conversation, saying he'll see me at the gym. As we leave, Lannette mentions how she hates when people say they know her, adding that she may know of him, but she doesn't really know him. I tell her it's no biggie and change the subject. "I hate for this wonderful weekend to end, but are you ready for this drive?"

"Unfortunately," she replies.

The trip back to Grand Rapids was quiet. I was hoping we were both thinking the same thing—when will we see each other again. When we make it to Tami's apartment, I walk her to the door. Shannel is inside shouting to us, asking if we had fun. She's grabbing and gathering their things so they can also be on their way back home.

"So, can I have your address so I can write you or something?" I ask. "Maybe I might even surprise you with a surprise visit."

Lannette smiled as she got out a piece of paper for us to exchange addresses. It was hard having to actually say goodbye. I hug her and kiss her softly. We kiss one more time and then I say goodbye loud enough to Shannel and Tami to hear me. I hug and kiss Lannette again for a final time.

"Don't be a stranger, Dre."

"I could never...I don't want to forget your beautiful smile."

As we part ways, she tells me to drive safely and I say the same. As I get to my car, I'm happy and sad at the same time. I'm happy because I met a beautiful young lady who understands me and likes me for who I am. But will the distance hinder us? I want to think positive on this one and believe that it will, proving the non-believers wrong. Stevie Wonder brings me back into Muskegon. I'm just chilling and feeling good in knowing this is a weekend I will never forget.

Chapter 5

(Everything Is Lovely)

It’s three weeks from the night since I met Lannette, and everything is on the up-and-up. It's been about two weeks since I've seen her, but we've been talking on the phone constantly. There’s not a day that goes by that I don't talk to her. We miss each other a lot. and that's all we say to each other when we are on the phone. I wish we could see each other, but it's alright. Hearing her voice is just as pleasant. I call her at work when I go on my breaks. And as soon as I get home, I'm talking to her since I took the block off the phone. The phone bill is probably going to be pretty high, but I don't worry about it; when I get the bill, it's probably going to be a different story. I don't care though—Lannette got me going. We're the perfect match and we have that combination that nobody else can unlock. This is the best that I've been feeling in a long time. I finally found someone I can relate to, and we're on the same page. Everybody at work is happy for me. My mother and father are also. Most of my sisters are happy for me except for Jillian; she is a hater. But deep down inside I know she's fine with it. I wouldn't care anyway because Lannette is one of a kind and I don't care what anyone has to say. Our distance only makes our hearts grow fonder and stronger for each other, so people can say what they want. I have a good vibe about Lannette that's making me weak in the knees.

At my job we've been working a lot of Saturdays. But lately we've been catching up on product, so one weekend soon I'm going to surprise Lannette and go see her. It's almost the end of July. Since we've met, time has just flown by. We've learned a lot about each other. I'm anticipating what will take place next. We're mature also enough to realize that Rome wasn't built in a day. I don't put a time on love, but it takes time to build that special relationship that makes love last and hold strong. We're both on the same page and ready to turn it to the next chapter of holding hands. Everything is real lovely now.

After a rough weekend of overtime, I called my friend Ronald up the following week. I wanted to see if he was going back home for the weekend. I thought maybe I could follow him back to Benton Harbor. It's been awhile since I've seen Lannette, and I can't wait to see the look on her face when I surprise her. Ronald confirmed that he was going home, so this was my opportunity to take that drive and visit her. The anticipation is endless. I keep picturing her pretty smile. This week of work leading up to the weekend went by slowly. When my coworkers asked me what I was doing the weekend, all I would tell them was that I wouldn't be in Muskegon. Friday had come and the day was going by pretty slow, so I decide to take half the day off using a vacation day. That way, I could be on my way to see Lannette. I put in a vacation slip and at 6:00 p.m. I was gone. There was no turning back.

I get home, shower, and put my gear on before calling Ronald to see if he's ready. Five minutes later we are heading south on 31 to Benton Harbor. He was driving kind of fast, so it was kind of hard for me to keep up, but I did. It usually took about one hour and a half to make it to Benton Harbor. At the rate we were going, it only took an hour. I didn't care because that way I would have more time with Lannette. Soon as we got into Benton Harbor, Ronald was rolling through the hood showing all his friends how good he was doing in Muskegon, showing off one of his new friends...me. Not being familiar with Benton Harbor, I'm being cautious because I heard a few stories about this place. So, I'm on my P's and Q's. I know they are not familiar with my car or me, so I say a little prayer and just go with the flow of things. I flat-out just want to see Lannette, but Ronald is the type that likes to boast and show off. We ride and eventually stop at a house where some of his friends are standing. I'm being cool, calm, and collected as possible, but I'm thinking, "*Damn!*" cause I'm anxious. He gets out and give his boys pounds and hugs. They immediately recognize that I'm not from there. They like my car and give me pounds too, though. After that, I am more at ease. Ronald introduces me and it was all good from there. We chat with his friends for a little while and begin back on our mission. We drive around some more and then we stop at his father's house. I was alright by then, but I finally let Ronald know that I'm tired of riding around and ready for him to show me where Lannette stays. He shows me the apartments where she lives and leaves me there letting me know it's cool to give him a call if I need anything.

This is the moment I've been waiting for. I walk up the stairs to her place and see a lady in a car looking at me. I nod toward her and continue to walk toward the door. I knock but I don't get an answer. The lady in the car gets out and ask me who I'm looking for. When I say Lannette Gates, she tells me that she is her cousin and that Lannette's down at Shannel's. She walks down to get Lannette for me, while I wait in anticipation. Moments later, Lannette comes running out toward me.

"Dre!" she screams, overwhelmingly.

"Hey honey," I respond.

Lannette runs up and gives me a big hug and kiss. "What are you doing here?"

"I'm here to see you, man."

"How did you find me, though?" she asks.

"Well, I already had your address, remember? And then I had a little more help from Ronald," I explain.

"Ronald," Lannette says with unease. "Oh well, it's good that you're here anyway. Give me another kiss."

I didn't waste any time giving her that. Lannette explained that the lady in the car was her cousin Pam and motioned her to come over to them.

"Okay, I was wondering because she was watching me close at me as I walked up to your door," I say. After a brief introduction, Lannette and I go into her apartment.

"Well, this is it, she says happily. "It's not much, but it's mine."

"It's nice; I like it," I say. It wasn't a real big apartment and it wasn't the bomb either, but it was hers and she was happy. That's all that matters.

"Demond is asleep; otherwise I would let you meet him."

"That's alright, Nette...we'll meet later."

"I can't believe you came up here to see me," Lannette says.

"I had to—I couldn't wait any longer to see your sexy and pretty smile, shape, and that walk."

Lannette begins to smile and blush. "Stop it, Dre!" By this time, her son wakes up and comes out his room squinting his eyes. "Hey baby," Lannette says to him. "This is Dre."

He says, “Hi” in a low tone and I respond with, “What's up, man?” He's still a little sleepy but I notice how deep his voice is for his size.

“Do you want to play with your toys?” Lannette says to him, which is all he needed to hear. His eyes immediately light up with excitement and he runs off into his room, but then he comes right back out with a Batman action figure to show it to me. Lannette looks at me knowingly with a smile as if to say, “See, you two are hitting it off pretty well already.” I smile back at her before turning my attention back to him, asking him about his Night Glow Batman. Everyone is happy, smiling, and getting along.

“I need to go grab a few things from Shannel's...I was doing my laundry. I’ll be back in a few minutes, if that’s okay?”

"That's fine, Nette, go right ahead,". I reply. She goes out the door, and Demond and I continue to play our hearts out. He even brings more toys out and all kinds. The more we play, the more I can see the joy and happiness in his face. I'm enjoying playing with him too. When Lannette walks back in after a little bit, her eyes get big seeing all the toys everywhere.

"We just got a little toy crazy, that's all," I say, as she smiles.

"I haven't seen Demond this happy in a while," she says. We continue to just enjoy each other's company until it starts to get late and it's time for her to get Demond ready for bed. As she does that, I'm thinking how everything about this woman is beautiful. When she comes back out to give me her attention, I can't keep my eyes off of her. I hate to end such a beautiful day on a dry note. As Lannette and I talk about planning something for next weekend, I can't keep myself from leaning over and kissing her.

“What was that for?” she asks.

“Just for being you,” I answer.

We hug and kiss a little more. The room begins to get warm real fast.

“I better get ready and get out of here,” I say.

“You don't have to leave, Dre. You can stay here with me,” she offers.

“I didn't bring any other clothes with me, otherwise I wouldn't go anywhere.” She gives me the softest and most gentle hug that I'll never forget. By this time, it's hard as hell for me to leave. “Maybe I can come see you next weekend or whenever the next weekend comes that you and I both have off.

"Sure, Dre...that will be fine."

We both get up and begin to walk out toward my car. I can tell she doesn't want me to go. I don't want to be impatient and we not take our time preparing for what's yet to come, so I choose to head home. Who knows, next time might be even better. Next time I might stay. If it happens, it happens. What is meant is meant. Everything is everything. When we get to my car, we sit on the hood and talk a little more. Saying our final goodbyes, a few girls walk up; one is a little hysterical.

"Lannette, have you seen mom?"

"No, I haven't seen her,"

"Alright can I use your phone?"

"Go ahead, Meek. Oh Kameeka, this is Dre," Lannette introduces us.

"Hi, I'm sorry I'm in such a rush. We're trying to get to the movies," Lannette's sister says.

"No problem, I've been there before, and it's nice to meet you," I say.

"And oh, this is my best friend, Karen," Kameeka adds.

"It's nice to meet you too, Karen."

"Same here," Karen says to me.

Once they leave, Lannette and I get back into our mushy mood, not wanting to let each other go. "Well Dre, until next time," she says softly.

"Yeah, the anticipation only makes the heart grow fonder," I respond. Lynette and I hug and kiss one last time. After that, I watch her walk into her apartment before I drive back around by Ronald's father's house to ask for directions back to the highway and say goodbye. I keep thinking about how I want to go back to Lannette’s, but a brotha’ got to get home. I leave and head for the off ramp, picturing Lannette, Demond, and I being one happy family. I hope that's what the future will hold. Anything's possible. It's up to my father up above. After this night that is now gone, I must say everything is looking lovely.

Chapter 6

(Put No Time on Love)

Another week at the plant, another Monday. I'm coming off such a wonderful weekend and it's hard to come back to this place. There are bills to be paid and things to buy. I don't have that big of a responsibility. I help out at home as much as I can, and my parents appreciate that. Then there's Lannette and Demond. Over the time we've been talking, I've grown feelings for her that I thought I never would. Her little boy, I accepted him from the first time she told me about him. I know he's not my responsibility biologically but that comes with my involvement with his mother. If I'm with Lannette, I must accept her child and I'm cool with that. I can't hold back my feelings for her.

It's been three months since we met, so by this time I should be able to express the way I feel, but I'm afraid I'll say it too soon. I can't care about that though. If you love someone, you love him or her flat out. Who says there's a certain month, day, or week when you figure that out? Can you really put a time on when you think you love someone? If you know, you know. Whether you know two months after you meet a person or the day you meet that person, if you love them, you love them. You're the only person who knows. I love Lannette and I can't even front about it. And whether she accepts it or not, I must let her know. The time chips away at the job today and it seems that way because I have something to get off my chest. At 6:30 I will be heading to the nearest phone to tell her that I love her. The result might be good or might be bad, but I must let her know. Soon as you know it, the time rolls around and I head straight to the phone, no lunch or nothing. I call but there's no answer. The rest of the night my throat is in knots because I know when I called on my last break that she should have been home by then. When 9:30 rolls around I'm off to the phone once again. I call and this time she answers. “What's up, Nette?”

“Hi Dre, what's up?”

“Oh, nothing really. just thinking about you, that's all,” I answer. She goes on to ask me about work but she seems to pick up on my tone.

“Why do you sound down?” Lannette asks.

“I'm not, I just have a lot on my mind,” I reply.

“Well Dre, I'm here to listen.”

“Yeah, I know, it's just not that easy. Well, it's easy because I mean it. I just don't know what the reaction might be.” She gets quiet and doesn't respond. “Lanette are you there?”

"Yes, Dre, I'm here. What's wrong? What do you have to say?"

"Nothing," I reply. "Well it's about time for me to get up out of here." I change the subject as quick as possible, but not realizing that the subject was literally still stuck in my memory bank. "I'll call you when I get home."

"Alright Dre, drive home safe."

"I love you," I say, not realizing it.

"Sounds like you said the L word," Lannette says.

"I did, Lannette. I do love you and I can't hide it."

"Are you sure?"

"I was sure when I first laid eyes on you. I knew you were the one and I have to express that," I say.

"You don't think it's too soon for love?" she continues questioning me.

"Is it a certain time when you supposed to love someone? When you know, you know. Did Romeo and Juliet put a time on when they knew they loved each other?"

"You're right. I just want you to be sure."

"Nette, I have never been so sure in my whole life."

"You are such a sweet and special man, Dre. I'll stay up for you as long as you want me to," she replies.

"Look at you, don't make me drive up there tonight," I reply.

"Maybe for the weekend?"

I got quiet for a minute. Inside I was lighting up like Christmas candles. "Sure, hopefully I don't have to work. If I do, I'm not going in."

Lannette giggles. "Alright Dre, I don't want to keep you from going home. Call me when you get settled in."

"Bye, Lannette. I love you,"

"Bye, Dre. Drive safe."

As I hang up the phone, I feel good getting that off my chest. I just hope that one day eventually she will feel the same.

When I reach home and finally get settled in, I call Lannette again. Our conversation was brief, but I can tell she wants to see me pretty bad. I made plans to see her this weekend whether we have to work or not. I don't want the distance to seem like it's a problem. It wasn't, but if work is mandatory, I have no choice but to work it or blow a point. After work Saturday. I'm heading straight up there. No ifs, ands, or buts about it. When I get to work the next day, no one is scheduled to work Saturday overtime, so I'll be Benton Harbor bound. I call Lannette and let her know I'll be there the weekend. She seems excited, which is a pretty good sign, and I feel pretty good also. To be blunt, I can't wait; I'm anxious but nonchalant about it. Today flew by and the weekend was in effect, and I was ready to be 31 South bound. I gather my things early Saturday morning, got the car ready, and told my mother and father I'd be back Sunday or Monday before work. It was depending on if everything goes smoothly, which it should. This is my first time going to Benton Harbor solo, so I'm praying everything will be fine. What is meant is meant, I always say.

The drive went smoothly as I play Frankie Beverly and Maze. I'm feeling real relaxed at the moment. Driving off the Benton Harbor exit, I finally make it to Lannette's apartment complex. I pull in front of her apartment getting a chill in my body. It was a good feeling though, making it to Benton Harbor safe knowing that I'm about to spend quality time with a beautiful woman that I care a lot about. A woman who I'm not afraid to say I love. She's everything to me. I knock on the door hoping that she's up already. Lannette answers the door right away and greets me with a kiss and a hug. The day is already starting off on the right note. Demond is with his father for the weekend. I tell her I hope she didn't send him to his father's because I was in town because I enjoy playing with and getting to know him and would like to spend time with him as well. She smiles and explains that Demond wanted to go with his father. I thought that was special and remind Lanette not to feel as if she has to push him away because I was there. I didn't want her feeling as if she had to put me before her child. No woman should do that, and if they do, they don't have no respect for themselves or their child.

After our heart-to-heart talk, we realized that we had a real understanding for each other. We always seem to be on the same page and that was a plus on both parts. I got my things squared away and we were ready to enjoy this beautiful sunny day together. This day was basically getting to know the town, as well as visiting her friends and family. The sight of the town wasn't really much to look at. Certain parts were better than others. We decide to drive her car, which was cool. I really didn't want any unnecessary attention to my car. I'm not from here and I'm not packed with a gun either. I just thought it would be best to drive hers, this being my first time being in the heart of the town. Benton Harbor is small, similar to Muskegon but smaller. It is more crammed, more agitation, and more crime. I used to hear stories about this place. The whole time we were driving, it seemed like everyone we passed grilled us real hard, which is expected, Lannette and I being the beautiful couple that we are and all. I don't mean to brag or boast about it; we're just that type of couple. As we drive deeper into the heart of the town, things are looking real grim, almost like a ghost town. We drive to their downtown area, but there wasn't much to see. I'm thinking to myself, *"Who will want to remain living in the town with no hope and nothing to look forward to?"* Then I thought about Sinbad, the comedian, who was born and raised here in this town; Ernie Hudson, who played in Ghostbusters and Penitentiary II. I heard that Vivica Fox was from here too. From a town that doesn't show much, it did have people with talent and a gift to do better for themselves. I guess those people didn't want to be trapped in with nothing to look forward to. Some people might like living here, but I couldn't. I'm not judging anyone. Where I'm from isn't all that great either but it's home; just like Benton Harbor is home to Lannette, and I love her. I wouldn't care where she stayed. I'm driving 100 miles to see her, not the town.

As we check out more sights and areas away from the hood, Lannette looks over at me and ask if I was okay, in which I nod my head yes. The whole time we drive, Lannette looks as if she wants to just leave this place, and I can relate to the way she feels. I feel the same way when I'm back in Muskegon. Wanting to get away and escape from the bullshit that the town is always feeding you. Then we begin to talk about making power moves or just starting over, moving on to something better and leaving behind what we want to forget. The only reason she's still living in Benton Harbor is because of her mother and that is understandable. Those are some of the same reasons I'm still at home and because of my job. I really don't feel like I accomplish anything at my job, except for fixing up my car, as well as buying some clothes and jewelry.

Material items are nothing like a big house or business. People always tell me I'm still young and have time; not to rush things. I'm just a person who won't stop trying to get what I want. If I don't have this type of attitude, no matter what age I am, I would never accomplish anything. I express this to Lannette and she agrees, pointing out how she sees that I seem to know what I want out of life. I tell her I also want her in my life. I know it's meant for us; we wouldn't be together this moment if it weren't. Lannette looks at me and pulls me closer to her. Her expression on her face looks like she doesn't have a care in the world. We may look crazy being this close to each other in the front seat of her car, but so be it. I'm beginning to sink deeper into her heart. As we discuss the things that we want out of life and what we want out of each other, we are on point in all aspects. Honesty, friendship, and understanding are enough for the both of us. I'm thinking about more than that; I just want to really get to know her. Time begins to fly as we drive around the town. Lannette and I begin to make each other laugh as we crack jokes on each other. We're bonding and even Stevie Wonder can see that. Then we begin to talk about her job at the hospital, which she says is an okay job, but she would like something better. I compliment her on everything because she's doing it on her own. She really doesn't have a lot to offer a brotha' in regards to material things. I mean, she isn't struggling or nothing, but her car isn't all that.

The main criteria I look for is if the person is at least working, going to school, or striving for something better out of life. I could care less if she works at Burger King, McDonald's, or lives in a shack. As long as she has self-respect, strives for something better, and doesn't stop at what she's trying to accomplish because it's not all gravy. Finally, an appreciation to others when they help out by returning the favor is nice too. Lannette fills that position in my book. We finally decide to swing by her mother's house, but her mother ends up not being there when we arrive. We then go by her older sister's house, Mary, who is engaged. Lannette tells me a few things about her sister's fiancé, Harry. She says he's cool but he's not the best looking person in the world. Looks aren't everything either, I tell her. A person can be as beautiful as ever but have an ugly attitude, which she agrees with me on that. We get to their house which is in a pretty good and quiet neighborhood. Her sister and her sister's fiancé look to be doing pretty well for themselves. He has a Jeep Cherokee that's in mint condition. It's a 98, a brand new car. Mary has a Tracker, which also looks nice. She was at home, but Harry was with a friend. Lannette and her sister Mary resemble each other, but Lannette has the advantage like a tennis game. Mary is nice, showing me good hospitality, and she's talking about her job. She doesn't talk about her engagement much or her fiancé. She mentions having a friend in the NBA that played for the Hawks, but that's about it. She talks with a country accent almost, real proper. I enjoy conversing with her because she's nice. We finally decide to leave and try to catch her mother, but we still have no luck there. Lannette wants to then take a few of Demond's things over to his father's house, so that was our next stop.

The day is beginning to almost come to a close. As we reach her baby daddy's house, it seems to open back up again. It is still light outside, so Demond and his father Clarence are sitting on the porch. I can see him watching me. I expect that, but I bet he isn't expecting me to get out of the car with Lannette. As we both get out of the car, I wonder what is going through his head at this point. Lannette says that he has committed himself to God which is a very good thing to do and also a big step. I'm not trying to rub nothing in this face by getting out with Lannette, so I introduce myself and say what's up to Demond. Clarence responds, introducing himself and gives me a pound. He seems like a cool cat. I head back to the car to let them finish up their business. No showing out or harm intended. Lannette gives Demond some more of his things and then we're on our way to her apartment. The day has flown by like clockwork. It was a good day, a very good one. The day is over, but the night is still young. As we pull up to her apartment, her mother was pulling out. She pulls back in when she sees us and greets us with a big smile. Her mother is real nice, real down-to-earth, and I like her right away. She's funny, has a good sense of humor, and a real sweetheart. She goes on about how Lannette and I look nice together, blowing both of our heads up. We're speechless. I love it though, it's easy to know when you are around good people. Lannette tells her mother day that we went over to Clarence's house and they laugh about me getting out and introducing myself. Her mother jokes, saying that I was letting him know there was a new sheriff in town. I laugh along with it and agree. Her mom stays for a good minute talking with us, then she decides to leave, telling us not to do anything that she wouldn't do. Her mother is real kind and I enjoy talking with her.

It's 10 p.m. but we're not tired so decide to hop in my car and take a ride down to this special spot she knows of. Here we sit on the benches and just hold each other. This is a Kodak moment. We're by a harbor just looking at the water and taking in everything. Love is definitely in effect. Lannette wants me to sing to her. I didn't think that was such a good idea, but she pleads with me to do it, so I get brave and give it a shot. She smiles, kisses me, and holds me tight. At this moment I'm beginning to get a little aroused by her sweet kisses and her warm body next to mine. We make our way back to her apartment. Today has just taken its toll on us. We both were in a Love Jones, as they say. As we get into her apartment, her friend Shannel comes down from her place with her little boy Isaiah. They came to see if Demond was home so they could play at her apartment for the night. Lannette tells her that he is with his father. Shannel seems agitated when mentioning Clarence's name, but when Lannette retells her the story of me and Clarence's introduction, Shanell loves every bit of it. She gives me high-fives and gives me props. What I did wasn't a big deal in my book, but I figured Shannel figures that whatever Clarence did to Lannette, she's happy to see it happening to him this time around. After Shannel leaves, I jump straight in the shower. I put my smell goods on afterwards. Lannette says she just loves the fragrance. “You just smell too good. What are you trying to do to me?”

“Nothing honey, you know I got to smell good though. You don't want me to smell bad,” I answer.

When Lannette goes to take a nice soothing bath, I get my boxers and tank top on. I look around the apartment and go into the kitchen to be a little curious. With my height, I can see above her cabinet. I look on top and I see some pictures. I take them down and begin to look through them. There were a couple of pictures of Clarence and her mother. Towards the end there were pictures of Lannette in some lingerie. Damn! All types of shit started rolling through my head. I have to admit she was out cold. I heard Lannette finishing up in the bathroom, so I put the pictures back, go to the couch to sit down, and turn the TV on.

"Are you all right in there, Dre?" Lannette yells from the other room.

"Yes sweetie," I respond. When Lannette comes out, she has her smell goods on too and a sexy nightgown. All I can think about is those pictures. I'm trying my best not to get besides myself. She kisses me. "I have something to show you, Dre."

Aw shit, I'm thinking. I'm not prepared for this. At the beginning of the day, sex was the last thing on my mind, but now it's all I can think about. I can control myself though, I've been disciplined this far. Lannette goes to the kitchen and gets the pictures. I'm thinking I already saw those, although she doesn't know it, I don't think.

"This is a little something me and Shannel were playing around doing last week." She shows me the pictures and describe what she was thinking as she was taking them. Now at this moment, I begin to get real aroused. To be frank about it, I was brick-hard, woody, or whatever you want to call it; I was there. I change the subject quickly and tell her I'm tired. We both decide to go to bed or try to at least. I had too much on my mind to sleep. "Dre, you can sleep in the bed with me this time. Demond's not here," she says.

I take a deep swallow and respond, "Okay."

We lay down and she turns the lights off. Lannette then asks me for a goodnight kiss, so we kiss softly and slowly. I don't want to stop. We roll to our sides facing the opposite direction. I can't help but see those pictures in my head while smelling her sweet fragrance right next to me. I can't help but to try to steal another kiss. "Lannette," I say quietly.

She turns my way and says, "Yes, Dre?"

"Can I have another kiss?"

"Yes."

We move close to each other. The one more kiss turns out to be one long kiss and another, then an even longer kiss. At this point I'm thinking if I should I press it further or not. I'm trying my hardest to think with the bigger head, but both heads at this moment are agreeing with each other. I move on top of Lannette in full salute, and she feels it right away. She begins to get aroused. She's passionate but so quiet, soft, gentle, and nonchalant. At this point no actual lovemaking is taking place. Just my body on top of hers, and we're breaking all the boundaries there are to break. I press my manhood to her special spot. She begins to accept me more and more. At this point there is no turning back. Then my conscience gets to me. My big head breaks the ice. "Do you have any condoms?" I asked cautiously, not wanting to ruin the moment.

She hesitates for a moment but responds, "Damn," in frustration of us stopping.

I'm thinking to myself do I want to go through with it. It took me one second to think "hell yeah" in my head. I do love her, I do care for her, and I can spend the rest of my life with her. As she is retrieving the condoms, I'm now wondering if she is a freak or a whore for having them. Or is she responsible for having them? Something must be wrong with me because I'm thinking at this moment. The average Joe wouldn't give a damn. She comes back in the room with the condoms and gives them to me. We begin to continue where we left off, but my conscience was eating at me. "Lannette, I say in a gentle tone. "When was the last time you did something like this?"

"About six months ago or maybe longer," she answers.

"With who?"

"Demond's father," she replies.

"That's nothing compared to how long it's been for me," I say.

"How long for you, Dre?"

"Do you really want to know and want me to be truthfully honest with you?" Lannette looks into my eyes and nods her head.

"One summer ago," I answer. She looks at me with a confused look. "I was waiting for a special woman like you," I continue. "A woman I care for and a woman I love." There was nothing else to talk about between us. We were both fully unclothed. I made sure the condom was on properly. This was the moment I had been waiting for. I take a deep breath and slide my manhood in gently. Then she wraps her legs around my waist and the rest is history. It's quiet between us as we lay holding each other afterward. I break the silence. "Lannette, what's next with you and I?"

"What do you mean by that, Dre?"

"I mean, you know. We're a couple right?"

"Do you think I would have allowed you to stay with me this weekend if we weren't? You wouldn't even be next to me right now," Lannette confirms.

It's something I've been waiting to hear all day and night. I feel good at this moment and wanting Lannette the more we talk and look at each other. We begin to kiss again, picking right back up where we left off. The next morning, Lannette and I are all smiles. She and I are joking with each other about last night's events. The weekend is coming to a close with me having to work the next day and Lannette having to work today. It's still early and she contemplates calling in. I tell her it won't be necessary. I don't want to be the cause of her not going to work. We take our time getting out of bed. We're joking with and kissing each other. Luckily, she doesn't have to be to work until 5. We decide to pick right where we left off the night before. We finally get out of bed, go shower, and dress. I'm preparing my things to take them to the car, wishing I didn't have to. We still have some time left to spend with each other. So, we drive around and pick her little boy up and drop him off at her mother's, who is watching him while Lannette goes to work. Demond is happy to see us when we pick him up. The next time we can all spend some time together. I say goodbye to Lannette's mom and her sister Kameeka, and then I tell Demond that we will do something together next time I come. Our birthdays, mine and Demond's, are so close to each other and around the corner. I tell him I will do something nice for him.

We then drive to her sister Mary's place so I can meet Harry. When we arrive, Harry is outside washing his truck. He looks me up and down as Lannette and I approach him. She introduces us and we give each other pounds. We both say it's cool meeting each other. Harry talks about how he has been to Muskegon once, but his experience wasn't pleasant, but it was a long time ago since he'd been there. All I know, he seems pretty legit. He has a legit job and Lannette's sister as a future wife. The cat was a pretty big boy. I'm talkin Notorious BIG status, but he did have himself intact. He has a crib, nice truck, and a fiancé. I congratulate my man for taking care of his business. He was looking at my car and told me I had it fixed it up pretty nice. Everything was gravy. We talked about hooking up the next time I came to town, and I tell him I'm down with. Then it's time for Lannette to go to work. We tell Mary and Harry goodbye. Now comes the hardest part of the visit – leaving. The weekend was so lovely. Both of us enjoyed the love that was created and the love that has become one. We've been seeing each other and we both seem to feel the same about what took place over the weekend. Nothing was planned or staged. Everything that happened was meant. Whether it was a month from when we met, three months, or even the year; maybe even three weeks after; love is love and you can't put a time on it. Lannette and I drive back to her apartment. She has a few more things to do before she goes to work. I can see it in her eyes that she doesn't want me to go. I tell her that the next time I'm going to stay longer, and she tells me she likes that idea. We were in love and like I said before, it wouldn't take Stevie Wonder long to see that. As we hug and kiss each other goodbye, I realize that Lannette is the only one that really understands me and has grown to love me; that's real. No matter how long of a time or how short of a time, when you fall in love with someone, it comes right when you need it.

Chapter 7

(Most Memorable Times)

After that lovely intimate weekend Lannette and I shared, there were more weekends that we shared. The intimacy grew stronger with each time. Lannette and I had reached the level that the average married couple wouldn't expect to reach. Lanette have spent so much time together over the months. It's sort of like we stay in the same town. Saying goodbye is always going to be the hard part, but when the weekend comes back around, I'm there. I hardly know what Muskegon looks like anymore. I work second shift, so I'm at work all day. When Friday night hits at 10 p.m., I'm headed to Benton Harbor to see Lannette and Demond. I have gotten so close to her family, it's like they're my family now. Being with her so much and seeing her mother and sisters every weekend I'm in town, this is our relationship at its best so far.

Everybody loves me, from her mother, to her sisters, to her friends. Even her sister's fiancé Harry seems to be cool about me visiting. I have been spending so much time up there, people have started getting the impression that I stay there. My mother and father have begun to miss me a lot because I am never home. My sisters and brothers are wondering what has been going on with me. My friends assume that I moved out of state because no one sees me anymore. There wasn't anything in Muskegon for me. Lannette and Demond are in Benton Harbor. I want to be wherever they are. I am serious about this relationship and I have no other ties with any other woman. I don't want any other woman. The only lady I want to give my all to is Lannette. She has the key to my heart. Lannette loves every bit of me when I show up each weekend. What time we do have with each other is everything and what we share is memorable and can never be replaced.

It's moving closer to our birthdays—Demond's and mine. Lannette and Shannel are throwing a party together this upcoming weekend to celebrate Shannel's son's birthday as well. I want to make sure I'm there so that I can be there for Demond and to help out with the party as much as I can. A friend from work named Angelo, and myself, drive up that weekend. I want to go by myself, but since it's Demond's birthday and he's having a party, I figured he and his mother should share the day and night together. I don't pack any clothes this time and I figure it would be alright to take a friend since I'm not going to sleep over. We make it to Benton Harbor in an hour before the party. Lannette, Shannel and I aren't quite finished with setting for the party at the park. Lannette has been up real early today and it shows. She is still beautiful and always smiles regardless. I introduce Angelo to both ladies, then we're ready to go to the park with the rest of her family who's up at Lannette's apartment. I can see frustration on her face, so I try to be as helpful as possible. Lannette's sister, Kameeka, says there was a hole in one of her tires. They needed as many cars as possible for all the kids going to the park. Now I really see and understand the frustration on her face, but I tell her not to worry. I tell her to continue finishing up what she has to do, and I'll take care of her tire. I tell Kameeka to follow me to the nearest tire store. We make it there on time just before the place closes, then get her tire fixed and squared away. Now we're all ready to go to the park and enjoy the festivities.

Demond was already there with Lannette's mother and Clarence. As we all pulled up, Demond's eyes lit up. He was happy to see all the people and all of his presents. Isaiah, Shannel's son, was pretty excited as well. Lannette, Shannel, and her mother seemed bothered by Clarence sitting at the table, but I told Lannette to be nice and to not let it get to her. She agrees and we begin goofing off and playing with each other a bit, hitting each other's butts, and kissing. My friend Angelo can see we care a lot for each other and begins laughing at us. Lannette was looking good today. She was just smiling and being herself. Lannette and Shannel decide to let Demond and Isaiah open their presents. They were happy and pleased at what they got. I had bought Demond some shoes and he received a lot of educational books and games from his family. Isaiah received some of the similar things that Demond received. After all of the "oohs and ahs" of the presents being open, everyone got their grub on. Some of the children begin playing and enjoying themselves. My friend Angelo is talking to Lannette's mother, Lannette has disappeared to Shannel's car, Kameeka went to my car to listen to Al Green, and Demond, Isaiah, and their young guests were at the playground with Clarence, so I was sort of by myself. I decide to have a little talk with the Clarence. As I walk towards him, suddenly all eyes seem to be on us.

"What's up?" I say to Clarence.

"How are you doing?" he responds.

"Lannette tells me that you're saved? I think that's wise and a big step to take—not an easy one," I say.

"It's all about what's in your heart, Dre. If you allow the Lord to enter your heart, he will override any doubts that you have."

"Yeah, that's true. I'm feeling what you're saying." Clarence seems pretty cool. All in all, the conversation was about him committing himself to God and people in church. Sometimes I wish I had stayed in church, which I share with Clarence, who tells me that it's never too late to go back. I agree. As our conversation begins to come to a close, we began walking back towards the others. I respect him for not being the typical baby's daddy by acting an ass and showing off and shit. He was cool about the situation. I have a lot of respect for a person who has respect for himself and learns from his mistakes. Clarence also shows me the same respect and he ends the conversation by saying that Lannette is a good girl. It let me know that he was real about the situation and was not holding any grudges.

As we walk up to the rest of the crowd, Demond and Isaiah come running up behind us. Lannette points her finger at me, gesturing for me to follow her. "What did you two talk about?" she asks when we're alone.

"Nothing really," I answer.

"What's nothing?"

"About church and all that. That's about it you. You know, male talk and all that."

"I thought I was going to have to come down there and get some things straight?" Lannette replies.

"No, nothing that serious. It's all gravy," I say.

Lannette smiles. "Alright, I didn't want to have to get rowdy for a minute," she jokes. We blow a couple of kisses at each other as we begin to clean up the area and gather all the gifts Demond received. We all headed to Lannette's apartment, not expecting everyone to come, but they did. That included Demond, Clarence, her cousins, her cousin's kids, Shannel, Isaiah, her mother, Kammeka, Angelo, and I are all in Lannette's small apartment. She looks at me and gives me a crazy look. All I can do is chuckle to myself. She's smiling at me the whole time. She comes over and whispers in my ear, wishing we could have some alone time. I tell her the feeling is mutual. We all watch Demond and Isaiah open some more gifts, eat some cake, and then people eventually begin to roll out. Clarence and I shake hands before he heads out. Shannel and Isaiah say their goodbyes. All of the cousins and their kids start wandering outside to play. Kameeka and their mother go outside as well. So, we all just decide to enjoy the rest of the sun before the night begins to fall upon us. We take pictures and I play with Demond's and Lannette's little cousins. It was a nice day for a birthday, having fun, and getting closer to Lannette, Demond, and the rest of her family. Lannette's older cousins are getting better acquainted with a blunt session outside. Everything was everything. Lannette and I really didn't have a chance to share any special moments. Just being there with her, Demond, and her family was a special enough moment to satisfy me.

It's nightfall and everyone finally says their last goodbyes. Angelo and I are ready to head back to Muskegon. We go back inside to Lannette and I help

Demond put his gifts and things away. Lannette and I go to her room and share a little kiss and hug before I depart. We talk about spending the weekend in Grand Rapids for my birthday next week and going to a comedy show. That should make it more exciting. I give Demond a goodbye hug and Lannette a kiss for the last time that night. We both hate that I can't stay, but next weekend we'll make up for that. Angelo and I are Muskegon bound and dread the weekend because it's one day away from being over. We have to go back to work on Monday. It's all gravy. We both enjoyed ourselves on this beautiful and memorable weekend.

Monday is here sooner than you knew it, since Sunday flew by like it was on crack. Angelo and I see each other at work and talk to a few others telling them how we enjoyed our weekend. The work week goes by and my birthday falls on Labor Day, which is Monday of the following week. That means a three-day weekend, which means more time for me with Lannette. I make reservations for us at the Holiday Inn in Grand Rapids. I'm at home gathering my things for this wonderful birthday weekend. My pockets are looking full. I rent a 98 Cherokee with the six-disc CD changer. I really don't like renting something I can't have, but it's my birthday I don't think it's a bad idea. My father is implying I must be moving again, based on all of the things I'm packing in the truck. I bring my VCR and CD player too. I want this weekend to be special for Lannette and I. I also want this weekend to be memorable and enjoyable. My mother shakes her head as I finish packing my things, and she ask me when will I be back. I tell her Monday or Tuesday the day after my birthday. She hugs me and tells me to drive safe, then I'm off to go pick up my baby Lannette on this beautiful Saturday morning.

I'm cool, calm, and collected as I let the sounds of Jay-Z's "Streets is Watching" soundtrack bringing me in safely in Benton Harbor city limits. "It's alright," I repeat a song lyric that plays as I pull up to Lannette's apartment. *Everything is alright,* I say to myself. I'm about to enjoy a wonderful birthday weekend with that special young lady who stole my heart. I give her a kiss and a hug when she opens the door. "You all set?" I ask her as I walk in.

"Yeah, Dre. I'm all set."

"Where is Demond?" I ask, looking around for him.

"He's with Kameeka," she replies. "She's going to watch Demond the whole weekend here at my place."

"Oh, then I can see him when we get back."

I grab Lannette's bags and take them to the truck. Now we're ready to make the best of this wonderful weekend. With it being my birthday this Monday, this is the best birthday gift I could ever receive. Lannette compliments the truck I rented, and I share with her how I wish it was mine. As we ride smoothly on the highway, Lannette and I are both in the zone with no interference from anyone.

We make it to Grand Rapids safely and pull into the Holiday Inn's parking lot. Lannette and I are looking and smiling at each other, remembering our first weekend we spent together here. We check in and it's still early, so we decide to get a bite to eat and go see my sisters and my niece in Ann Arbor. My older sister Hillary has been staying there for over seven years and my youngest sister Joy just recently moved there with her two kids. Lannette is my right-hand woman and all in for it. I have over 1,000 miles to get rid of on the truck I rented, so I thought I might as well put it to good use. We have about a good two hours before we will touch down, but Lannette and I kept the ride interesting. I tell her about my sister Joy who got out of an abusive relationship with her baby's daddy, who she had been with for six years. The whole time she was with him he had been like that, but no one noticed it. My sister was fed up with it and moved with my other sister Hillary, who has no kids, and she takes care of her business. Now she's helping my sister Joy out in the process. Lannette thought that was nice of Hillary to do that and made a comment about men being abusive. I let Lannette know that I wouldn't ever hit her, but maybe shake the hell out of her. We both laugh. We are on that level and can joke like that with each other. We drive, joke some more, talk about her past with her baby's father and the turmoil he put her through. It's hard to believe someone would do those things to such a beautiful young lady like Lannette. I tell her it was his loss and my gain. She smiles at me and reaches over to kiss me on my cheek.

After an interesting two hours talking and joking, we make it to Ann Arbor. I can't find where my sister stays right off hand, but we find the place eventually. Soon as I pull up, I can see my two nieces looking down at me from their upstairs window yelling, "Uncle Dre, Uncle Dre!" My sister Joy greets us at the door, and I give her a big hug and introduce her to Lannette. My nieces are running down the stairs with their arms stretched out for a hug and telling me how good they are doing in school and how much they miss me. They meet Lannette, telling her how pretty she is, and Lannette is telling them the same. They all smile from ear to ear. My sister Hillary was at work but arrives shortly after. Hillary is the greedy one out of the family and selfish sometimes, but she has a good heart.

Sometimes it's a very rare that she shows it, but she does. Hillary and I have that off and on relationship. One minute we are joking and cracking on each other, until I get the best of her and she gets mad. All in all, when it comes down to it, we love each other to death. As soon as she walks in, she's already in a joking mood, asking me what I was doing there. I respond, "Not to see you!".

She laughs it off and we do the introductions. They both say it's a pleasure to meet one another, and then it happens the moment we all sit down and talk. Hillary starts telling Lannette about my childhood. Hillary is always trying to embarrass me any chance she gets. Joy just agrees with her and laughs. I can't do nothing but laugh because my sister is telling it all. Lannette loves every bit of it. I wasn't going to go out like that, so I begin to tell some of the things Hillary did when she was younger. We all are having such a good time laughing as

Lannette gets to know them. This is a memorable moment and I love every bit of it. After all the jokes and laughs, it has to end sooner or later. Lannette and I are ready to be on our mission to Muskegon to meet some more of my family and just enjoy the rest of the day. We tell my sisters and my nieces goodbye, and I tell them that we had a nice time. As soon as we get in the car, Lannette looks at me and laughs. She can't believe how bad I was when I was younger. I was a handful back then. I keep her laughing all the way to Muskegon, telling her incidents of when I was a kid, and she can relate to it. Lannette shares that she wasn't the sweetest kid either. We make it into town, and we decide to go see what my brother Jeff is doing. I knock on the door and he peeks out looking at us with a crazy look on his face.

"Open the door," I shout.

Another look and Jeff finally opens the door. “Oh, I didn't know that was you he,” he responds.

“That's a rental car. This is Lannette, my boo,” I say as she smiles.

Jeff introduces himself before I add, “Well we was just stopping by to see what you were doing. We're about to go visit some of the folks before going back to Rap.”

“Do you have a room over there?”

“Yeah. I'll be back Monday probably,” I answer.

“Alright, Dre,” Jeff says, then turns his attention to Lannette. “It was nice meeting you.”

“Same here,” she says back to Jeff.

We had a good time on this Saturday being on the highway laughing and joking. We drive by my sister Brittany’s and my cousin Erica's. I introduce Lannette to my family as my fiancé. My sister, her kids, and the rest of my family are all over Erica's. I had forgotten that it was Erica's birthday on Friday, and they are throwing her a party today. Everyone loves Lannette, who looks at me and shakes her head. She's looking at me like, "What have I gotten started." She is cool about it though because we're having a nice time. Robbie, my gay cousin, is making Lannette laugh. She's almost in tears. We are having so much fun and it just flies by.

We started our day at 10 a.m. and it was already 9 p.m. The highway took half of that time. All in all, this day, or should I say night, has been the most fun I've had in a while, and having it with Lannette was all the better. We have a big event ahead of us tomorrow, so we decide to tell everyone goodbye and then we make our way back to my mom's and father's before we eventually depart and arrive in Grand Rapids. We are both tired from being on the highway, laughing, joking, and having a good time. It took some energy from us, but it was worth it. We are still joking about the earlier things that took place. Once we get to the room, Lannette and I are ready for a nice shower and the bed. Waking up the next morning, was the best part. She and I both look at each other and enjoy every moment. Today is the day of the comedy show and one day away from my birthday. I'll be turning the big 21, and I'll finally be legal. Lannette and I finally get out of the bed to get dressed and ready to enjoy another beautiful day together. We start off at the mall just walking and talking. We sit and chat for a little bit. I see a couple of people from Muskegon that I know who are going to the comedy show later on that night. We decide to walk in some of the stores. We go into a jewelry store and talk about what kind of diamond she would like to have when she gets married. Lannette says it didn't really matter as long as it's from the heart. I thought to myself how I would get her a ring that sparkles just like her smile. I do love her with all my heart—she's one of a kind.

We left the mall to catch a movie and get something to eat afterwards. The day went by fast but was more laid back than yesterday. We went back to the hotel to get ready for the comedy show. We showered and got spiffy. Lannette has on an outstanding black fitted dress, which makes my skin crawl just thinking about how good she looks in it. I let Lannette know when the night is over that she is going to pay for wearing that dress. She smiles and takes it as a compliment, which it was, because she was looking tight. Lannette compliments me, but I am too busy with my eyes locked on her. I could care less about me. We are both happy to be with each other and hold our heads high when we work together. We make it to the comedy show, and it is wall-to-wall in this place. Lannette and I are excited to see Joe Claire, the comedian off of Def Comedy Jam and Rap City. We walk in and it seems like all eyes are on us, but it's cool though. I see my coworker Jim and his girlfriend Tish. Jim was with me the night I met Lannette, so he's happy to see us together. We talk to them for a little while and then we head to find our seats. The show is hilarious so far, but we sneak away for a minute to take some pictures. The photographer is cool as we're having a laugh or two on how he's telling Lannette to stick her butt and hips out some more when she was posing. It was a special occasion, so I buy one picture with "Happy Birthday" and the other saying "I Love You". These are two pictures that I'll always be remembered. We went and enjoyed the rest of the show. Joe Claire stole the stage by a long shot. We get our money's worth and then some. After the show, we drive around a little bit, but Lannette and I have other plans to attend to.

When we get back to the hotel, I shower first then she gets in the shower. Lannette has a complex about me seeing her unclothed. I thought I would stand on the opposite side of the bathroom door and surprise her when she came out. Lannette knew something was up. She decides to call out my name to see if I have the lights on. Soon as she opens the door, she peeks around the opposite corner and there she is stone-ass naked. She sees me hiding then jumps back in the shower and slams the bathroom door. We both laugh for a good five minutes. When she finally comes out of the bathroom again, I tell her she looks beautiful and she shouldn't hide her overall beauty. Let's just say was 5 a.m. was when we finally went to bed. We had to wake up soon after to check out of the room. We woke up later and shook our heads at each other, because we were still tired and wanting to stay in bed. Lannette leans over, kisses me, and tells me happy birthday.

"Oh yeah," I say. "I almost forgot. I'm legal." And it was just in time. Next month I will be going to Las Vegas with some of my friends from work, a trip that I have planned months ago. Lannette and I shower, get dressed, and check out on time. As we were about to leave and head to Benton Harbor, Lannette wants me to open her gift she got me. She got me a nice shirt, a Docker's pants outfit, and a nice card. I give her a big hug and kiss, telling her the best gift she gave me this weekend was her love, understanding, and companionship. That was the best gift ever. She smiles bright and we kiss once more. I hate for the weekend to end. This was the most memorable and greatest birthday that a 21-year old can have. It didn't take us long to make it to her apartment in Benton Harbor. I almost wish Benton Harbor was further from Grand Rapids because I just didn't want us to part ways so soon. We both need some rest and to get ourselves prepared for another workday that's ahead of us tomorrow. I bring her things in the apartment, and Kameeka and her friend Karen in the living room. Demond is running out of his room to hug us. After some small talk with Kameeka and her friend, Lannette smiles at me as I prepare to leave. The weekend was unbelievable. I hug he and tell her we will spend some time together another weekend. She hates for me to be there for such a short time, but all good things must end sometime. Lannette and I discuss the next time we will see each other, as she walks me to the truck and kisses me so soft and gently. This was a special moment and I hated for it to end. I told her I would have something special for her on her birthday which was three months away. This is a woman who came into my life and stole my heart. I can't go wrong with her. We kiss again for the last time and she wishes me happy birthday again. I will never forget this day. After walking back to go inside, Lannette turns around and looks at me and says passionately, "I love you, Dre."

I just about cried. It was so innocent, so pure, so meaningful. I walk up to her and pull her in for a hug. I don't want to ever let go. This moment fulfills my birthday wish.

"I love you to, Lannette."

I begin heading north to Muskegon. I'm driving along in total silence; no music, no radio, and just Lannette on my mind. I just hope that the future holds the best for us, maybe even marriage. Only time will reveal. I make it home and pull into the driveway with the sun still shining bright. It reminds me of Lannette. How great her smile is and how much she brightens up my day. I feel so young, I feel so complete. I just turned 21 today and most say I'm too young to fall in love. I don't think so because if I were even 30 years old when I met Lannette, it wouldn't really matter. I think the only thing that matters is that we both love each other, understand each other, and best of all we became closer friends in the process. This was one of the best weekends I could have ever experienced in my lifetime. At the age of 21, it will be the most memorable.

Chapter 8

(The Down Times)

In a relationship you have good times, bad times, ups, and downs. Lannette and I stayed having good times and up times throughout the whole five months we had been together. We never argued, all we had was fun, laughter, and understanding for each other. At one point in our relationship, the tables turned. Things began to get rough for a minute. Seems like second-guessing and people started to get jealous of our relationship. Things that are so petty that you would never think that could hurt anything, but it does. I guess this was a test of how much we really loved each other. I knew it was meant for us the day we met. There was no question about it. I guess you can say Lannette and I made some bad choices and situations began to go downhill.

Lannette was getting tired of the job she was doing at the hospital and decided to switch to a factory job. She has a cyst on her hand, and it will pop if she puts a lot of strain on it. The factory required a lot of strain on her hands because they made lamp shades. Lannette already quit her other job at the hospital, so now she was stuck at this factory and it was wearing her hands out. Things weren't working out for her and her hands were constantly in pain from making the lamp shades. Lannette said enough was enough and quit the factory with no other job to go to. She realized that she made a bad choice by switching jobs and was beginning to get in a bind. She was falling short on money and it was hard for her to pay the rent. Lannette mentioned to me the only thing that kept her going was that she had me in her corner. I tried to help as much as I could, but my situation wasn't looking spectacular either. After my birthday, I wanted to buy a truck since I was still staying at home and didn't have many bills. Ever since I rented that Cherokee, I wanted one. Now I regret that I did. I didn't have any real responsibilities until I got that truck with a $323 truck note that I had to pay every month. Now I regret I even bought the truck. I hated to see Lannette down and out. I wanted to help her as much as I could by any means. This was a real test for us, and we needed each other now more than ever. I began to work a lot of overtime at work doing double shifts at a time so I could maintain payments on my truck and help her out too. It was making me tiresome and stressed at times, but I had to do what I had to do. I didn't want this situation to ruin our relationship, but it seemed that the further time moved along, the more grim our relationship got.

Sweetest Day was coming up and a real close lady friend of mine named Ella was getting married on that day.

Ella didn't think it would be a bad idea if Lannette and I came to the wedding to take our minds off of things. We decide to go. It's raining pretty hard outside and it's not so much of a beautiful day but Lannette and I manage to make it. I know Ella will be pleased to see us. Ella is a woman who always understood where I was coming from when it came to being involved with someone. She felt what I was going through because she has been through it too. It's always helpful coming from a woman's point of view at times. Women are hard to understand and Ella was there for me when I needed to know different things. She's a down-to-earth lady, the kind of lady who will have your back and will be there for you no matter what; a real sweetheart and close friend who knows the meaning of friendship. Her husband-to-be is a very lucky man right now because he's about to marry a very understanding friend as well as a caring wife. Lannette and I wait patiently as they are still preparing for the wedding and running behind schedule. I begin to ask so many questions about marriage, including if I were to ask her to marry me at that moment what would she say. Lannette hesitates for a second and that bothers me. It was no question in my mind she would say yes right off back. As the wedding begins, I just sit quietly wondering to myself, if she loves me the same way I love her. I never thought about that much because I thought we both were on the same level when it came down to it. Lannette tries to talk to me during the wedding but I don't respond. I am in shock in a way but disappointed most of all. I'm trying to get some things together in my head, so the situation won't turn into an argument. The wedding was beautiful, and it was coordinated beautifully as the bridesmaids and groomsmen all came down the aisle. Ella and her new husband said their wedding vows and it was a very sentimental moment. After the wedding was over, Lannette could tell that I was upset because I wasn't responding when she was trying to talk to me. Everybody was going around shaking the hands of the bride, the groom, the bridesmaids, and groomsmen. Lannette was upset and she didn't want to walk in front of me at first. All the groomsmen were looking at her closely, drawn to her looks, as we walked by shaking their hands. I had enough of that and told her to get in front of me. Lannette was trying to do that on purpose but I wasn't having it. As we got to the bride and groom, I could see Ella giving me that look. I shook her husband's hand and Lannette was shaking Ella's. When I got to Ella, I reached out to shake her hand but she pulled me in to hug her. It was all gravy, I thought, because we had a friendship like that.

As we began to leave, I tried to break the ice and try to talk things out. I apologized and she apologized but

I’m still disappointed by her hesitation earlier. We had gotten deeper in conversation about marriage, including how she and Clarence were about to get married at one point in time. That was new to me. She never mentioned that before. Now I'm really wondering about her feelings toward Clarence.

“Do you still love him?”

“I don't care for him anymore,” she says.

I’m trying to take her word for it, but it's not that easy. All types of thoughts are racing through my head. Was I too blunt, did I fall in love too quick, was I sweating her too much, was I losing her? Does she still love me? When we made it to her apartment after our drive from the wedding, it seemed like we flew back because we made it back there so fast. I think it was because I was angry and ready to shed tears. I didn't want to ruin what I had in store for the rest of the night. It was supposed to be sweet and regardless of the way that I felt about it, I still love her very much. I couldn't hide or cry about it. Lannette was feeling pretty bad about the way I was feeling at the moment because she wasn't being upfront with me. I still can't believe she never told me that she almost got married. When we get in the apartment, she hugs me and apologizes once again. I don't want to argue anymore. We hug and kiss each other. The situation is in the back of my head for the rest of the night and I prepare a beautiful dinner for us. I bake chicken, cook Stovetop, macaroni, and cheesecake for dessert. It was a nice dinner for two. Regardless of what went on today, the night was beautiful. Lannette and I enjoyed the wedding even though we didn't talk during it. We both recognize our own faults and embrace each other at the end of the night.

I have to go back to work on Monday, and the following weekend I will be in Las Vegas. Her sister Mary comes by and I was telling her about my trip that I was going to take the next weekend and how much I wished Lannette could go. After Mary went home, Lannette mentioned to me how Harry questioned her about me going to Vegas and why I wasn't going. He said that I was going for the women and the partying.

"Lannette, I love you too much to worry about any other woman. My main purpose of going is to win some money, get away for a minute, and get my mind off of things. I wish you could go." It seemed like every time we spent a weekend away from each other's hometown we got closer to each other's heart. I also wondered why Harry was so concerned about what I was doing. He hardly knew me. I thought he was pretty cool, so why was he trying to spit venom on me. Lannette added that he criticized me up and down after he met me, claiming that I was a nigga selling dope and probably had three different women. Even if I did, that's my business, not his. I didn't check him about shacking with her sister and not being married. I didn't criticize him about his clothes because I could care less. He is six years older than me and I know he has better things to do than to criticize me. I told Lannette that I didn't sweat it and when I got back from Vegas she wouldn't have to worry about anything. I was going to try to make something happen for us. She smiles at me, gives me that look, and kisses me gently.

I went home the next day and got my things prepared for the next work week. I thought about church, how much I was missing it, and how much I needed to start going back. I always pray to God no matter what type of situation I'm in. Whether it was good or bad, as long as you keep Him first, everything will go as planned. The work week came and went until it was time for the trip. I spent the night over Rick's house the night before I went to Las Vegas so we could ride to the airport together from his place. Rick was the cool guy at my job who had just gotten a divorce from his wife. He was doing well by himself and taking care of his responsibilities. I always seem to pay attention to people who went through something and how they manage to go on. I was hoping to myself that I would never have to go through it. The other guy who is going to Vegas with us is Alfonso, an older guy, real cool; he makes me laugh. You need people like that around you take your mind off of things.

The whole night I talk to Lannette on the phone. She's telling me she might have to move back home with her mom and Kameeka until she finds a job and get back on her feet. She doesn't want to do that, but she might not have much of a choice. I tell her not to worry and I will try to help as much as I can. Before we hang up, making our kissing noises over the phone, I tell her I love her and Demond and will miss them while I'm in Vegas. She wishes me a good time and tells me that she loves me. I pray that I will win something big or if not, just being away will be fine. The next day we're on our way and we make it to the airport safely in Detroit. Now comes the hard part – Las Vegas. I have never flown before so course I am a little nervous. The guys don't make it any better, making me more nervous saying how my ears will pop and how bad the turbulence will be. When we get on the plane, I make sure I have my Bible with me. I'm going to read it all the way to Vegas. As the plane begins to move, Rick and Alfonso look at me to see if I am okay. They laugh at me for a minute because of the way I'm looking when we take off. Once we get in the air, it isn't smooth sailing. I read the Bible all the way to Vegas. I want to be wide awake just in case things don't go right. I also want to read different scriptures too. We land safely after it took only three hours to get there. The weather is a lot warmer and all we can see when we get off the plane are slot machines and dollar signs. We walk through the airport to go pick up our luggage. Forgetting about the NBA lockout, it doesn't cross my mind that the basketball players are here in Vegas. We see Derek McKee who played for the Indiana Pacers right off the bat. It didn't seem believable at first, but it was him. We continue to get our luggage and things. My mind begins to wander looking at all the lights, slot machines, and hearing the "cha-ching" of money dropping. This was a place where either you win it all or lose it all.

I had a friend in the Air Force that was stationed here in Vegas. I plan to give him a call to try to see him before we leave. The city is unbelievable, and I call my mother from my cellular phone before the shuttle takes us to our hotel. I tell her about all the palm trees I see, the big casinos, and how I'm digging Las Vegas like a grave. After I hang up with my mother, we make it to the hotel. My friends from back home told me to have a game plan and to not get caught up in the glamour and lights, and to make wise decisions. They also told me to eat wisely. The steak and eggs are the cheapest meals that will save me money. The first day being here I took that advice. There was a three-hour difference from back home, so it seemed like we were up forever. We got a bite to eat were ready for fun and gambling after that. We hit the casinos. We all just started out on the slots trying our best to win big, but no one was lucky yet. I wandered off to place some bets on some football games, and then went to the crap table. It was different from how we usually play, so I just looked on until I went back to the slots. Rick was doing alright, and I figured Alphonso was not having much luck either.

Time flies when you try to win big, and it was still early in Vegas. The time difference has us all off track. We decide to call it a day. Nothing big happens and no one wins big. We go back to the hotel. Rick and I are planning what casinos to hit up for the next day. There are too many to choose from. We decide to just sleep on it for the time being.

I call Lannette and tell her I'm having a good time. I also tell her that I miss her and Demond. She tells me that she misses me also and that she will be moving with her sister Mary and Harry instead at the end of the month. The momentum shifted about 360 degrees. She said that they said it was cool and this would give her some time to get herself together. I tell her to be strong and that I will try my best to help out as much as I can. I tell her I will be there the weekend before she moves. Now I really have to win big, I think to myself, and I have only three days to do it in. The next day, Rick and I don't wait for nothing. We're both on a mission. We need to hit big. I find Alphonso lollygagging, so I leave him behind 'cause we have no time to waste. Rick and I go to the Stardust Casino on the Strip. It was live on the Strip. Seeing different cars, you never seen before, it was amazing, but I had no time for that. It's time to win big. Rick hit the slots and I hit the roulette table. I play $5 a game and I am winning until I get greedy and put $20 on the game and lose. Then I keep losing, so I decide to move to the crap table where people are betting hundreds, even thousands, on games. I knew that I was out of my league.

I find Rick, and he is winning. *Damn!* I say to myself, thinking I need to get busy. I begin to pray for anything I can get. I win $80 and Rick tells me to cash out, but $80 isn't enough; I want more. *Be smart*, I was thinking, but I lost it all back. Rick shakes his head while he's on a roll. It was all good though—at least someone was winning. I begin to think about Lannette and not being able to see her on the weekends like I used to. I have to do something. I go to the ATM machine, which is something I said that I would not do while I was in Vegas, but I was beginning to get into a slump seeing everyone win but me. I get $100 and press my luck but nothing big happens. Rick came out all right and even gave me $50. I couldn't thank him enough for that. It helped me out a lot. Rick was cool and a good friend. After that we decided to go to a different casino across the street from the Stardust.

I have never has seen so many bums on the street in my life. As we walk, we grab a bite to eat, gamble some more, and place some more bets on some football games. We gamble our hearts out, but nothing big happens, but we have two days left. I was thinking about pawning some of my jewelry to get some money. I was losing in a big way; Vegas wasn't everything I thought it would be. It was so easy to lose and so hard to win. We gamble some more before making it back to the hotel. My luck changes a little bit because I hit for $50 on the slot machine in the lobby off of a dollar. Rick and I call it a night and it is still early in Vegas, but our bodies are on our usual time zone and back home it's pretty late. I call Lannette again before I go to bed and we talk briefly before we hang up. I know I have to make something happen these next two days. We joke with Alphonso being a poor sport for not participating in gambling with us. I guess he has other plans, and it was cool. Rick and I are on the journey to win some long dough.

I call my friend Will the next day and he leave a message for him to meet me at the Stardust. That's where Rick hits big so that's where we went. As I find a nice slot machine, Will walks up to me. It was good seeing an old friend from back home, especially when we are both so far away. Will is doing well in Vegas. He's training to be an FBI agent. He was always smart when we were in school and now it's paying off for him. I congratulate him on this, and we began to talk about old times and about all the new friends he has met in Vegas. It was a cool moment and it took my mind off gambling for a minute. We decide to go get something to eat. This was the best part of the day to me, not worrying about gambling, money, and just eating. After that, we went to a few different casinos and did some sightseeing. We started talking about women, particularly my situation with Lannette. Will just told me to take it one day at a time, which I totally agree with him although it hasn’t been easy when you love somebody so much and they might not love you as much as you love them. We began to gamble a little more after our conversation at the MGM Grand to gamble, where they also have wrestlers, like Goldberg and some others for the kids. I feel like Will brought me a little luck because I begin hitting $80 here and there on the slots, but then, again, my luck took a slight change. The days in Vegas go by so fast. We begin to get tired after a moment. Tomorrow was Sunday, and Sunday is one day away from us getting on the plane and being back to reality. Tomorrow I want to buy some gifts for my mom, dad, Lannette, and Demond. Will prepared to leave, riding the buses back to his destination to get around. Rick and I walked him to his stop, and I tell him to be safe and continue to succeed, adding how inspiring and motivating he is to me. Finally, I tell him I will make sure I kept in touch with him and let his family know that I saw him and he is doing good.

Rick and I continue back on the mission to try to hit big quick. We left one after the other after having no hit, deciding to make one last try at New York, New York but nothing happens for us. All I can rely on are the football games that we placed bets on. Once we get back to our hotel, I'll find out what's going on with the games. I take a detour to the lobby to find Alfonso but I can't find him. Rick was already asleep when I return, so I shower and went to bed. The next day was slow motion. Alfonso told us about his night on the town and how he went to Planet Hollywood where he saw a few celebrities. We all decide to take it slow this last day in Vegas and buy gifts. Hopefully we will win some money by the end of the night. After shopping for gifts, we take our things back to the hotel and then hit the biggest casinos. I went my separate way from Alfonso and Rick, praying and hoping God would answer me. I walk the Strip and go to a couple of jewelry stores hoping that I can get a good price for my charm I want to sell. The starting price level I was given was bogus, so I decided to keep my charm. Instead, I saw a jewelry store like we had back home and looked at some engagement rings. I came across one that fit Lannette perfectly, so I had to have it. I asked them if they had the same ring at their location in Michigan, and if so, could I put something on it and make the other half of the payment later. We worked everything out and they let me take the ring that moment.

Just think, I was going to pawn something to get money, but instead I bought something that would benefit me and Lannette's relationship. I was planning on popping the big question on her birthday, which was one month and a half away. I catch back up with the guys later, not telling them anything that I did. I find watching the football games that we placed bets on. My teams aren't doing well at all, but Rick's teams were. *Damn,* I thought. *Another downfall for Dre*. The day was over, and the night took its toll. We hate the thought of tomorrow and having to get back on the plane to go back to boring Muskegon and back to work. It was fun while it lasted. Next time I'll be prepared for the worst when it comes to gambling. I guess I got my hopes up too high. I call Lannette as we start getting our things together to leave tomorrow. I tell her I had a nice time, but I didn't win big. I decide to tell her that I did get her something as well as Demond, and I will be there for the last weekend at her apartment before she has to move. We made our usual kissing sounds over the phone before saying I love you and hanging up. My night was restless after that and I couldn't sleep. Thinking about Lannette, Demond, and what the future held. It is already daybreak when I finally close my eyes, and now we had to make our flight. I was tired but ready to do what I had to do. I had fun and saw an old friend, so that was cool. As we got on the plane, I am not even afraid of flying anymore. From that moment on, I put my life in God's hands. No matter what I do and where I go, God is always going to be there. On the plane, I sleep all the way back to Detroit while Alfonso and Rick eat the plane's half-ass food courses. We land within three hours. Everybody was dreading going back to work the next day. It took us another three hours to make it back to Muskegon. Nobody won big but we all enjoyed ourselves and plan on going back next year. I tell Rick I appreciate the money he gave me and how he was there for a brother. Now it's back to reality. I walk in the house, put my things away, and prepare my clothes for tomorrow. It will be a short week since tomorrow will already be Tuesday. I give my mother and father their gifts and then I hit the sack. I was worn out from thinking myself to death. I didn't get enough sleep the last night in Las Vegas.

Through the work week I tell everyone about my trip and the fun we had, but the weekend comes up quicker than expected. Next thing I know, it's Halloween and I am on my way to spend the last weekend with Lannette and Demond at their apartment. When I get there, Demond runs to me to hug me, asking me where I've been. He told me he missed me and shows me all kinds of new toys he has. Lannette's apartment is empty. The only thing that is there is her bed and TV. I want to cry when I see the look on her face. I hold her and don't want to let her go. I tell her that everything happens for a reason and we will work it back to the way it was. Lannette was down but still happy that I was there with her and Demond. I give them their presents; Lannette loves her teddy bear with the message that says, "Somebody that was in Vegas loves me!" She likes it a lot. I bought Demond a light-up yo-yo and he enjoyed it. His father's mother picked him up for a Halloween party, which gave us some time alone to talk about some things.

She understood that I wouldn't be able to see her that much on the weekends with winter coming up.

"Hopefully by the wintertime, though, I will be back on my feet," she says.

"I pray that you will," I add. As long as we're together, that's all that matters to us. Lannette mentioned to me the only thing that will go wrong is her losing me. I tell her don't think that way and that it was meant for us to be together. We came too long of a way, which she agrees with me but I see the doubt in her eyes. All I can do is hold her. We fell asleep in each other's arms until the next day. We awake to shower and get dressed. I don't want the weekend to end but it came quickly.

Lannette has a few other things to move and I don't want to make it any harder for her than it already is by being there, so I prepare myself to head back to

Muskegon. We go to pick up Demond and I say my piece to him. I tell him to be there for his mother by being a good boy. I know it's not the end, but it's hard to let go of being able to see the people you care about every weekend and not being able to see them that often. This is the moment I dread. I tell her again that I will try helping as much as I can, and she thanks me for just being there in general. That's why I love Lannette so much because she is strong and understanding. We had some good times here in this apartment. As a matter of fact, we had some great times here. We embrace once again and it's hard to let go, but we have to. I tell her until next time instead of saying goodbye. I was letting her know that I will be around no matter who she is staying with. She smiles and we hug and kiss once again before leaving her there. I was out the door in tears. I couldn't hold it in any longer. It was bound to happen sooner or later. As I drive out of the parking lot,

I envision us one day being one. There's a saying that whatever goes up must come down. At this moment, this is more down than ever. I just hope and pray that the situation will work itself out, so Lannette and I can prove people wrong that long-distance relationships don't work. That also goes for those who pray for our downfall. When you are on top, that's when people want to see you down. Lannette and I might be down but not beaten.

Chapter 9

(Things Fall Apart)

All the bad luck Lannette and I were having, you wouldn't think things could get any worse. I jinxed myself when saying that because it has done nothing but gotten worse for us. I can't really put the blame on anyone or anything, but I began to start blaming myself for everything. Maybe if I would have never bought my truck, things would be right, and I could have helped with her rent. Things will be the same, I thought, and we would still be stronger than ever. If I had my own place she could come and stay with me. I thought of all types of reasons things were the way they were. When it comes down to it, everything happens for a reason, but I wasn't trying to hear that. I was doing everything in my power to make things work, but it seemed to get worse and worse. The thought of losing Lannette was on my mind constantly.

What was once the best thing that ever happened to me was now backfiring.

The first few weeks when they moved in with her sister and her sister's fiancé, our relationship changed for the worse. Clarence lived directly one block down from them. I didn't think much of it at first, but when she told me she put some of her things over his house, that got me to thinking, *"What type of shit is this?"* The only business they should have is business that deals with her son. Lannette and I really didn't talk as much as we used to anymore, either. Mary and Harry say that I couldn't call their house late. Mary didn't really have a problem with it, but it was Harry who had a problem. Lannette said that when we did get a chance to talk, Harry would be all in her mouth. We weren't even communicating on the same level anymore. Lannette was feeling so down and out about not having a job since a month-and-a-half ago, living with somebody else, and not being able to see me on the weekends anymore. Lannette was pretty much giving up on everything, including us, and she didn't have much to strive for anymore, so she thought. I just kept encouraging her to pray and to keep her head up no matter what happened; not to let the situation ruin what was meant to be.

Lannette began to allow Clarence, Mary, and Shannel to cut into our relationship. I pretty much didn't know what to do anymore. I begin to get sick, literally shaking at times. Not having anybody to talk to and no shoulder to lie on. I would write Lannette letters instead of calling her so much. Harry began to add his two cents about everything we were going through. He started showing his true colors about me, also assuming that Mary had a crush on me. I wasn't caring much about him though; the only person that I cared about was the young lady who stole my heart six months ago. Lannette would call me in the mornings before she took Demond to school. The talks were brief because she didn't want to run up their phone bill, having them bitching more than they already were. So, when she called me, she would hang up and I'd call her back. A week before Thanksgiving, our situation fell further.

I had been working a lot of overtime to maintain my truck payments, and it was wearing me down. I called Lannette on Friday, but she sounded funny like she was hiding something or just didn't want to talk. I let her know I was coming to see her the weekend, but I didn't let her know what time. The thought of her being with Clarence was in the back of my mind on occasion, no matter how hard I tried not to think about it. The weekend came and the night beforehand Lannette and I talked. She was acting shady towards me. I thought nothing of it. I figured she just had a bad day and it got the best of her. Clarence had picked up Demond that night. The next day came and I left early to go to Benton Harbor. It was a beautiful weekend, it being November, and it was pretty hot, and it was because of El Nino. As I drove down the street that Harry, Mary, and Clarence lived on, I saw Lannette's car parked in Clarence's driveway. I'm thinking two things: if she is in there, I'm going to snap; if she's not in there, what the fuck is her car doing here. Without thinking, I pull up to Clarence's house and start banging on the door not caring about nothing. I just want to know what the hell is going on. Clarence answers with a crazy look on his face like, "Nigga, are you crazy banging on my door like that?"

"Is Lannette here?"

"No, she's down the street."

"Oh, I see." I am a bit more calm now. "How are you doing, Clarence?"

"I'm alright," he responds, as Demond waves at me from the living room.

I leave then continue my way to Lannette's, Mary's, and Harry's house. Harry is outside looking at me close, then says, "What's up, Dre? Lannette is inside."

I walk straight in the house demanding an explanation from her. Lannette's barely awake, so I wait until she gets herself ready. We both sit down, and she can hardly look at me in the face. I know the outcome of our conversation will be bitter by the time I leave, but I prepared myself for the worst when I arrived. Lannette begins to tell me how she truly felt, like not being over Clarence when our relationship began. My eyes almost pop out of my sockets. I play it off like it's nothing, and I tell her to tell me everything that's on their mind. Slowly but surely she begins to tell me that Clarence had been calling her. He was trying to get back with her. He wasn't saved anymore, and he was blaming Lannette for it. I tried to tell her that that was bottom-line bullshit to mess our relationship up. Everything I was trying to tell Lynette was going in one ear and coming out of the other. The more I tried to reason with her, the further her mind was wandering. Then she says when we first began talking to each other, Clarence was still coming to see her. At first I think, *"Okay, because we weren't that deep into each other yet."* Then she put her head down and said quietly, "Dre, Clarence and I..."

"What Lannette, what?" I say loudly.

Lannette seems even lower at this point.

"What Lannette, did you sleep with him, huh?"

Lannette shook her head no and finally says, “He ate me out!”

I stay composed. “Is that all he did?” I say angrily.

“Yes,” she responds quickly.

I tell her I'm done talking to her as I begin to walk out the door. She tells me to hold on and begins to apologize. I sit back down, and we talk some more. I'm not upset; I just don't know how I'm going to react. I don't want her to see my bad side anyway, so I play it cool after a while. I tell her as long as she told me the truth, I was alright, and that she has to let Clarence know that she doesn't need him for anything. Their business should be about their son and nothing else. Lannette doesn't respond for a minute. “I need time to think.”

“I will give you as much time as you need.”

She then tells me she doesn't want me to call her for a while until she figures out what to do. It was hard for me to agree, but I want to show her I'm not sweating what she has told me. She is still feeling low, but I tell her everything is cool, and I still love her more than ever. I want her to go get herself together on her own. "Don't allow anyone to change your mind about us. Think for yourself," I tell her. "Advice is good, but the best advice sometimes is your own."

Lannette nods her head agreeing with me. All in all, I know she will come to reason later on. I just need to show her that I am not going for any shit. Either she wants to be with me, or she doesn't—it's as simple as that. As I begin to leave, Lannette hugs me and kisses me. Since we aren't going to spend the day together, I just decide to head back home. She asks me what I'm going to do later on, and I tell her nothing spectacular. I feel no emotion as

I'm leaving, and Lannette notices. She didn't think I would take it this well, I guess, but I prove her and myself wrong. I kiss her on the forehead, then I start leaving, bobbing my head to the music Harry has playing outside. Reality is sinking in at the moment. I talk to Harry for a few seconds, agreeing on how beautiful the day is. Everybody is outside washing their cars, and I was on my way back home. Before I leave out, I stop at Clarence's to see Demond. He wasn't too much for words when I stop by; I think he senses something was wrong, so I just give him a hug and tell him and Clarence to have a nice day.

On my way home, of course, Lannette is on my mind. Soon as I get home, I see her sister's number on my caller ID. I was about to call, but I thought I would let her think some more. By nightfall, Lannette is calling me again, explaining her side of the story and telling me how she doesn't want to lose me. I tell her everything is everything and I will always be around when she needs me. We talk for a while about her upcoming birthday. She has no idea what I have in store for her and I have no idea what the response will be. After we talk daily for a bit, everything seems like it's coming back on track. The week of Thanksgiving, Lannette has a couple of job interviews and she's calling me each day happier. I think we're back in stride full force, but after Thanksgiving, once again, things turn for the worst. My friend Ronald went home to Benton Harbor for the holiday. He told me that he saw Lannette and Clarence together at the mall. I didn't want to jump to any conclusions, but I was sure going to ask her about it.

I call Lannette and question her the following week after Thanksgiving. She can't deny it and says that she was at the mall with Clarence to get some Christmas gifts for Demond. I'm thinking to myself, *"Why do you have to go with him to do that?"* I ask and she gives me a story about he doesn't know Demond's sizes. *He doesn't know his own son's sizes?!* Something did not smell right to me. I was like Marvin Gaye and wondering what the hell is going on? Lannette and I talk all day and night. One moment everything is cool, then it's back to the same mess.

After we hang up, I'm distraught. I can't sleep, I can't eat, and all I can do is listen to sad shit like Brian McKnight, playing him over and over wondering does Lannette think about me anytime. I am sick, so the next morning at 6 a.m. I put my clothes on and head to Benton Harbor to try to work things out. I bring the engagement ring that I bought for her thinking maybe if I propose to her today, our relationship will shape up. I make it to Benton Harbor at 7:30 a.m. Harry's car is still in the driveway and I want to wait until he goes to work so Lannette and I can talk privately. I wait out in front for a minute, then Lannette comes out of the door looking in shock to see me. She motions for me to come inside, but I want to wait until Harry leaves. Lannette pleads for me to come in, asking me what's wrong, like she doesn't know. I finally decide to go in and Harry is looking at me like what's going on, but I think he knows what's up. We speak to each other for a moment while Lannette goes and gets herself washed up and dressed. Harry leaves for work after a while, and I have to get myself back on the highway in time for work before noon. It was 8:30 a.m. and I have three-and-a-half hours to get everything off my chest.

When Lannette comes out of the bathroom, she is looking at me like she's guilty of something. I ask her if she loves me, if she cares anymore, and what's the deal. She answers yes to everything, but she never looks at me. I have the ring in my coat pocket trying to decide whether I should propose or not or wait a week until her birthday and let things crumble some more. I'm looking at Lannette trying to read her mind. I'm wondering what she's thinking. Then I did it – I pull the ring out of my pocket, take off my coat, and kneel down on one knee. Lannette looks at me in more shock than earlier.

"Lannette," I say in a quiet, gentle tone. "I know we're going through some ups and downs, but I love you more than ever. I was going to wait until your birthday for this, but I can't wait."

Lannette's eyes grow bigger in size and she can't believe what was about to happen. I pull the ring out and she looks in more disbelief.

"Will you spend the rest of your life with me, Lanette?" She hesitates and I'm thinking, *"Please say yes, just please say yes."*

Lannette looks at me and shakes her head and responds, “I can't, Dre. I'm not right yet. I can't even think straight.”

I was crushed. My whole face would be pale if I was white. I was distraught, disappointed, and I didn't understand. All I can respond with is, “Why?”

She couldn't explain why, and I kept trying to reason with her; talking about all the things we did together, how to pray to God about me, and not taking what we have for granted. Everything was meant for us, I pleaded. Lannette wasn't budging on her answer and she said she had made her mind up. There isn’t anything else for me to do but drop some tears. I can't believe this is happening to me and my heart is crushed into bits and pieces. Lannette begins to put her arms around me to hold me, but that makes the situation worse. I question if she loved me enough to marry me. All she can say is she won't be committed to me like I would be to her. It was the nail in the coffin. I got up off my knees. By this time, Demond was awake and in the room. He runs to hug me, and I talk to him for a minute. He sees the ring in my hand and ask whom it's for. I pointed to his mom, so he takes it to give it to her. "Here mama,"

Lannette doesn't even want to take it but she does. I was about to head out the door until she stops me. "Wait, Dre. Stay right here Demond."

I follow her to another room to talk privately.

"Just think about it," I plead with her. "You don't have to let me know right away. Just keep the ring and think about it until the weekend." I give her another kiss and hug Demond as I head out and tell them I will see them the weekend. She pleads with me to take the ring, but I don't. I went through too much to get that ring, so I at least want her to enjoy it for a minute or hopefully forever.

On my way back to Muskegon, I cry my heart out like a bitch because I'm salty. I just don't understand how this is happening because I thought I did everything right, but everything went wrong. I hate having to go to work like this. I'm quiet as a mouse and not saying a word to anyone. Everybody is trying to figure out what is wrong, but I say nothing the whole shift. The weekend quickly comes around and once again I am on my way to Benton Harbor to see Lannette and see if she has had a change of heart, but there was no luck. It turns out Lannette told everybody about my proposal, including her best friends and family. Of course, Harry made a big deal out of it like everything else I've done for Lannette. She tells me he's asking about the price of the ring and how she should go get it priced and all that. Harry also added that he knew I was a baller and sold dope. I have better things to worry about than what everybody else's opinions are. I was still trying to work things out with Lannette. I told her to keep our business to ourselves, but it was too late for that. Everybody knew that the bridge was tumbling down. Lannette gave me the ring back and told me she couldn't go through with the proposal. I couldn't do anything but take it and accept what her wishes were. She said she still wants to see me and talk to me. I told her, "You aren't worthy enough to spend the rest of your life with me." I feel like a kid who just got his bike stolen or a crackhead trying to buy a rock with two cheeseburgers. I was sick and just downright ill. I was questioning whether Lannette ever did love me or just lust me. I can't call her a whore because she's not, but if she goes back to Clarence, what is she?

The same day I go to the mall to get my money back for that ring and decide to put that money from the ring on my truck payment. Fuck it. Why should I feel sorry for myself? It's not my loss. I can't deny that I am angry, upset, and don't quite understand anything right now. I need someone to talk to and the only person who really listened to me was Lannette. I decide to do something I shouldn't have by calling her best friend, Shannel. She was going through something herself with a guy from out of town. We were kind of in the same situation. I admit I shouldn't have talked to Shannel about the way things were going, but I needed to know some things that she probably knew about Lannette. She only said so much, but I got the picture. Lannette and Clarence had been with each other for five years prior to our relationship. Now I know how women feel when men dog them out. I didn't want to believe Lannette used me to get back at Clarence.

But the more I think about it, the more I want to confront Lannette about it. I tell Shannell that our conversation will be confidential. At this point, Shannel is more on my level. From jump, she knew Lannette was falling back into Clarence's trap. She was settling for less and lowering her standards. She only did it because her and Clarence had five years under their belt. Five years of lying, cheating, and verbal abuse; nothing compared to seven months of fun, laughter, friendship, and most of all, honesty from me. I played my part to the best I knew how to play it. That was just by loving myself, being true to myself, and respecting myself. For Lannette, she did none of those things. If so, we would probably be engaged by now and our relationship would not have ended before it started.

Lannette's birthday weekend rolls around and I'm going with the flow, so I plan to still spend her birthday with her. I try not to think about being intimate anymore.

That would make it worse on me. When a woman gives me a part of her, that means a lot to me, especially if being in love with that person. To me, the most precious thing a woman can give you is intimacy. This is sacred and this is a special moment between the man and woman. That word "love" can be simple as a kiss on the cheek or it can also be a kick to the groin. All in all, it's a bitch when it's taken for granted. But it's Lannette's birthday and she was feeling special because of her job situation, so I did everything I could to take her mind off it. Even though Lannette was confused about what was left of our relationship, I want it to work itself back to the way it was. I pick her up for a weekend in Muskegon MI and I want Demond to come also, but he ends up staying with Lannette's mother. Demond hadn't been the same either since the sudden move to Harry's and Mary's house. Lannette said Harry would mistreat Demond and talk bad to him. Harry started setting rules around the house for Demond and Lannette, which is crazy because Lannette is a grown woman. I think Harry is just jealous of her and us still trying to work things out, plus that engagement ring that I got her was bigger than Mary's. I think he's jealous of the fact that I treat Lannette better than he treats her sister. It's funny how a person can try to find so many things to mess the next man up and wind up looking like an ass. I try not to worry about other people's problems because I have enough of my own to deal with.

Lannette and I make it to Muskegon, and we check into a hotel. I tell her to get herself together, just relax, and take her mind off of things. Later on, we go shopping at the mall and I tell her to pick herself out something pretty. I try to make her birthday as pleasant as possible and us doing anything she wants to do for her birthday. After the mall, we go get something to eat. I want to take her somewhere quiet and where the food is prepared properly. Lannette just wants pizza instead. I can tell she had some things on her mind, but I make her laugh a little bit and try to take her mind off of whatever those things are. I go to the store, buy a bottle of hot sauce for the pizza, and A1 sauce for the steak fingers. Lannette laughs when I pull them out of my pocket at the pizza place. We are enjoying the moment, and after we eat we go back to the hotel to relax. As we both prepare for bed, everything is everything at this moment. There are two beds in the room, but I get in the same bed with Lannette to comfort and hold her. It starts out that way, but it ends up being something that I tried not to fall back into. We make love better than we ever had. It's better than the first time and it's unforgettable. I'm thinking after this that everything will pull itself back in perspective and be okay now. We're on our way, I thought, but I was just eating my own words.

The next day heading back home, she is quiet the whole way there. I keep asking her if she's okay and she tells me everything is fine. I know that something is bothering her, but I just can't pinpoint it right away. We make it back to Benton Harbor and I take Lannette to her mother's. Demond is waiting for his mommy and he's happy to see her. I talk to her mother for a little while. Demond doesn't even have three words for me, he's just happy to see his mommy. I say my goodbyes to them, and I go and hug and kiss Lannette goodbye, but she won't look me in my eyes.

"Nette, are you alright?"

"I'm fine, Dre." She puts her head down. I say goodbye to Demond and her mother, then I am gone. I'm on my way back home wondering what's bothering her.

Christmas is rolling around very quickly and we only have a week to go. My sister's birthday is coming up, so I have to get her two gifts. I rip and run getting everyone's gifts. On my sister's birthday, I decide to take Lannette, Demond, her mother, and Kameeka their gifts. I get Lannette a watch, some perfume, and some earrings. I get Demond a bike, her mother a robe and some earrings, and Kameeka a CD. I didn't get Mary anything because I didn't want Harry to take offense. I remember a time I wished her happy birthday and he got upset about it. Why, I don't know. Everything I did for Lannette and Demond, Harry had something to say about it. When he saw the presents I was bringing in for Lannette and Demond, he had a funny look on his face. When he found out I bought her mother and Kameeka gifts, of course he had something to say about that too. I have a funny feeling that he was up to something. Lannette tells me he tries to introduce her to his friends so they can try to talk to her. Some old hater shit! I don't sweat it though; I play everything off as nothing is wrong. His jealousy will smack him right back in his face in the long run.

I don't stay long when I drop the gifts off because it's hard for Lannette and I to talk since everybody is around. Living with Harry and Mary is kind of hard because those two are like 20/20, knowing all of your business and exploiting it. Before I hit the highway to head to work, I meet Lannette over Shannel's apartment. Shannel is at work; Demond and Lannette are spending the night there. He is still sleeping when I arrive, so that gives us some time to talk. She finally reveals what is bothering her all that time.

"I think I'm pregnant," she says softly.

I was quiet at first. “Don’t worry. If you’re pregnant, we're in this together, regardless of what happens for our relationship.”

We hug and hold each other for a moment. Demond wakes up and she begins to prepare him for school. After she washes him up and gets him dressed, him and I play for a few minutes before I take him to school. I tell Lannette to take it easy while I drop Demond off. When I get back minutes later, Lannette is sitting on the couch with her face in her hands not saying a word. I tell her not to worry about anything and that everything will be fine. I hold her close to me. We begin to kiss and caress each other. We both lay on the covers on the floor kissing and caressing until one thing leads to another; Lannette and I enjoy another intimate moment together. Under the circumstances, we don't think about it; we continue our relationship like it's never been falling apart.

It's past time for me to get out of there; I have less than 20 minutes to get into the shower and be out the door. I quickly shower and jump back into my clothes. Lannette is going to the doctor later to find out if she is pregnant, but I don't think she will tell me if she is. I kiss her goodbye, dashing out to my car. I hit the highway headed to work. I have less than an hour to make it. When I finally make it, I can't stop thinking about whether or not Lannette is pregnant and what will become of us. Will we continue being companions or will things really crumble? People say that when a woman has a baby, she wants to stay with the baby's father. But does Lannette still has feelings for Clarence? I'm beginning to think a 100-miles-a-minute, so I leave my work area to call her. She's no longer at Shannel's and she isn't at Mary's and Harry's house either. I'm thinking she's at the doctor's, but when I call her again on my break, she is still nowhere to be found.

Her mother doesn't have a phone, so I have to wait to hear from her. After I make it home that night, I call her again and she is still nowhere to be found. I'm hoping and praying everything is all right and I also want to know if I'm going to be a father. I think for a minute and pray that she's not with Clarence. I can't believe that, but it crosses my mind. After a couple of days, Lannette finally calls and says she's staying at her mother's, that's why she couldn't be reached. She had a lot on her mind and doesn't want Harry and Mary to find out anything. We talk but not for long because she has very little to say. She didn't go to the doctor, so she has no idea if she's pregnant or not. She tells me that her stomach hurts daily but that was it though. We hang up the phone without saying I love you or blowing kisses in the phone like we always do. Lannette is beginning to confuse me. One minute we're inseparable and the next minute she treats me like she doesn't know me. I try not to sweat it as much, but I can't think straight at times. I never been in a true relationship and now I'm feeling the effects of one going downhill. I don't know how I will react if Lannette and I break up and she has my child around somebody else. I began to realize that's probably how Clarence feels with Lannette and him after being together for five years. He's probably doing everything he can to get her back. I'm not there so I can't see everything; all I can do is leave it in God's hands, but I'm willing to do what is necessary. It's easy to go against His will. You really suffer the consequences when you do that, and the outcome will not be good. At this point, I really don't care about what happens to me anymore. If I can't have Lannette, I don't want no one to have her. I didn't realize how possessive I had become with her, and I just don't want to lose her. I haven't talked to Lannette since she called me the last time. I spend the whole weekend by the phone waiting to hear from her, but she never calls. I agree to not call her as much since she's staying with Harry and Mary, so all I can do is wait to hear from her.

The weekend passes and it is now the week of Christmas with all of the last-minute shopping, traffic, exchange of gifts at work, and, most of all, potlucks. After not hearing from Lannette over the weekend, I decide to pick up some overtime at work before they let us off on Christmas vacation. All the first shifters that I'm working with are asking me am I going to spend Christmas with Lannette and Demond, which I don't have the slightest idea because I haven't heard from her. Before my shift starts, I call her demanding an explanation. When she answers, I say, "Lannette, what's going on?"

"What do you mean, Dre?"

"You haven't called me, not even attempted to call me, so what's the deal with you?" She doesn't respond and she's silent, which makes me think she's hiding something or feeling guilty about something. "Cat got your tongue? Why are you hesitating to talk and why are you so quiet?" I continue with my questioning.

"Mary's here," she replies.

"Well go somewhere in the house where she can't hear you."

Lannette lets out a sound of frustration as it sounds like she's going into another room.

I tell her to just be straight with me, in which she responds and tells me that she went to South Bend with Kameeka over the past weekend to finish getting Demond some gifts and a new coat.

"You didn't have time to call or at least let me know something?" I ask. Lannette gets quiet for a minute. "What's wrong with that...is that all that you did?" I continue asking her.

"Yes, Dre."

"So just you and Kameeka went? Shannel didn't go with you?"

"Yes, Dre."

I didn't believe her. I wish I was there to see the expressions on her face. A person can get away with murder over the phone. "It's Clarence, isn't it Lannette?" She pauses for a moment. "Damn, why can't you see what he's trying to do? Are you that weak?" I say loud in frustration.

“Yes! Yes, Dre! I am that weak,” she shouts out. I stand holding the phone in disbelief of what I'm hearing. “I don't know anymore, Dre, I don't even care anymore.”

Lannette lets out her frustrations about being in this mixed-up situation and not being able to support her and Demond without Clarence's help. No matter how much Clarence has mistreated her, she always forgives him.

“What about me? What am I to you, a stranger?” Lannette doesn't respond to what I asked and that makes me snap, so I decided to throw dirt on her face that I should have left on the ground. “Just because Clarence sucked on your fucking clitoris, you're going cuckoo over his ass!”

Click. Lannette hung up on me and I knew I hit her where it hurts. I was just frustrated, angry, and I didn't understand why she was treating me the way she was. I immediately call her back, but I find myself apologizing to the answering machine. After I finally call back about five more times and leave messages, she finally picks up the phone.

"What, Dre?"

"I apologize for that but you're beating around the bush too much. Just be honest with me because you owe me that much."

"I have to go to an interview in a minute. We'll have to talk later," Lannette says dryly.

"When will we talk again?" I ask.

"I'll call you when you get home tonight, okay Dre?"

"Alright Lannette, call exactly at 10:30 p.m. I love you."

After I say that to her, she hesitates but finally comes to her senses and says it back. When we hang up, I think about how she didn't convince me that she did love me. The way things are going, I question if she ever loved me or did she ever love herself at this point.

I'm feeling all messed up the rest of the day at work. I'm not talking to anyone, I'm not eating, all I do is listen to my Walkman and try to work to keep my mind off what's going on. It isn't that easy though. My co-workers can sense something is wrong with me, especially Nick. He knows when somebody is going through something because he has been through it already. I just want to try to deal with it on my own now and if I need some advice later, I know I can go to him. When I get home after work, Lannette never calls, and it hurts me when she doesn't. At this point I am frustrated. I have to be at work on first shift tomorrow, so I'll just sleep on it for now. The next day I'm at work, and it's the last day before Christmas vacation for us. I don't say one word to anyone. Potlucks are going on around the whole shop and I'm not thinking about food, especially not this early. They have a potluck in my work area, and everybody is eating, laughing, and joking since it's the last day. Everybody on the line is asking me what's wrong and why I'm not eating. All I can respond to say is, "I don't feel good."

To tell the truth about it, I don't feel good because all I can think about is what's going on with Lannette. I have a funny feeling her and Clarence are together and that's all I can think about. The people on the line keep telling me to eat something but I just can't do it. When my shift comes around, I'm the same way; not eating and not talking to anyone. The day finally ends, and I go home to check my caller ID to see if Lannette called, but she didn't. I was really sick then, so I decide to call Shannel and she says she hasn't seen or heard from her. The next day I call her sisters and don't get an answer. It's one day before Christmas Eve and I at least want to talk to Demond before Christmas. Lannette is beginning to bring the worst out in me. I was really becoming fed up at this point. I've called around looking for her all day and haven't been able to reach her. By nightfall, I have decided to drive to Benton Harbor to find her.

There's only one thing on my mind and that is her being with Clarence. Why? Why would she want to be with him after all her and I've been through and accomplished together? When I make it to Benton Harbor, my first stop is her mother's house. Kameeka and I talk for a minute. She can sense that something is wrong with me because I have little to say about anything. I ask her about them going to South Bend but Kameeka responds, "I didn't go with Lannette to South Bend.

Lannette lied to me and it made me even more upset. I left immediately after she told me that. I knew who she was with and tonight I was going to prove it. I go to the mall looking for her, then over to Mary's. I don’t see her car. I was going crazy at this point and I’m driving in parts of town where most people wouldn't even attempt to drive in because of the crime. I don’t care though. I have to find out who is with her. I am hoping her and Demond are together. If Clarence is with her, I might lose it. I decide to stop by Shannel's and talk to her about what's going on and see if she can feel the pain I’m going through. She says she still hasn’t seen or heard from Lannette. I decide to sit and wait in front of Clarence's house for them. I know she isn't with anybody but him and I just have to see it for myself.

As I sit for a minute I cool down, but the more time has passed I begin to start getting agitated. It's going on 12 midnight. There is no sign of Lannette, Demond, or Clarence. Clarence stays a block away from Mary's and I don't see any activity or movement down at her house either. As I wait, I finally see Mary coming home from work and then Harry comes home shortly after. It's going on 1:00 in the morning and still no sign of Lannette and Demond. Now I'm getting upset. Finally, I see Lannette's car coming down the street and I'm steaming. They drive past me, Lannette isn't driving; Clarence is. I see her look directly in my face from the passenger side. I wonder how she's going to talk her way out of this one. They drive back by Harry's and Mary's, knowing, no doubt, that things can get ugly. Clarence gets out the driver side door. I'm still waiting and observing at this point. Lannette gets out of the passenger side and looks at my truck. I get out and see what her reaction will be. She shows no emotion, like nothing is wrong.

"Lannette," I scream her name.

"I have to take Demond in the house," she yells back.

She's trying to play me in front of Clarence and that triggers me to move closer. As I walk up, Clarence looks at me while she takes their son in Harry's and Mary's house. Lannette looks at me with a dumbfounded look on her face when she comes back out. I try to hold everything in as long as I can. Clarence gets some things out of her car and takes them in the house. I'm telling Lannette to come with me to my truck, but she says no. As Clarence begins to head down to his house, he is looking and listening to me go off on Lannette.

"What the fuck you mean no? What the fuck is up with that?" I shout at her.

"Let's go in the house, Dre?" Lannette gestures.

“I don't want to disrespect Harry’s and Mary's house like this. Let's just sit in the truck.

Lannette acts like she's putting on a front because Clarence is still close by and can hear her shouting. I am frustrated, angry, and louder than ever.

“Come on Lannette, what are you fronting for?”

At this point Mary is looking out the door with the phone in her hand. I don't know if it's the police or what. All I can picture in my head is being taken off to jail, so I plead with her to go with me to the truck once more. She finally does. I can still see Clarence watching from down the street as we get in the truck.

“What's going on, Lannette?”

“What do you mean, Dre?”

“What are you and Clarence doing, huh? I thought you weren't talking to him anymore.”

"All we did was go to South Bend to get Demond some more clothes for Christmas."

"Fuck that, Lannette...you didn't need him to go with you."

She gets quiet and I begin to see the frustration on her face.

"Why did you lie to me about the last time you went to South Bend?" I continue with my questions. "You went with Clarence didn't you?"

Lannette doesn't respond.

"Kameeka told me she didn't go to South Bend with you. You're busted and just admit it." She still doesn't respond and just sits there looking dumb in the face. Then Harry comes out the house and walks toward the truck. He opens the passenger door and ask Lannette if she's okay.

I'm thinking to myself, *"Of course she's all right because I wouldn't hit her for nothing."*

Harry begins to go off on me for no reason like he never met me in his life. "Why are you out here disrespecting my house, Dre?"

"What are you talking about, Harry? That's why we're in the truck."

"Fuck that, Dre! All that yelling and shouting isn't necessary. You are out here calling her bitches and shit. You don't have to do all that," Harry says.

"I didn't call her out her name, so what are you talking about?" I ask in disbelief.

"Just go before I get real upset."

"I apologize for yelling a little bit and if I woke you up from your sleep, but damn, we're in the truck, Harry!"

Harry grew more agitated and began to go off about how much money he paid for his house. At this time, I guess Lannette couldn't take the yelling anymore, so she gets out the truck and goes in the house, leaving me out there like a lost dog with Harry's big ass.

"Look, Dre...it's best that you just leave, and you deal with Lannette on your own time away from my house."

"So, it's like that Harry?"

"Bye, Dre. It's best that you just leave." He starts coming around to my side.

"Damn, it's like that man?" I say, still in disbelief as he gets angrier.

"You bitch-ass nigga, stop!"

Now, I'm sitting here thinking to myself that my mother didn't have any bitches. "What you say, Harry?"

If he calls me out my name one more time, it's going to be on. He walks back to his house and that's when I start my truck up.

"You better not be out here when I come back," he shouts back at me.

I have two choices: stay and wait to see what he's going to get or leave and still be in one piece. At this point I'm a little upset by what he called me, but I was by myself and I didn't have any weapons or protection. Clarence is still watching from down the street. I start heading down the street and pull up alongside Clarence. "I have no beef with you. Everything is everything," I say to him.

Clarence nods his head in agreement. "Did she tell you how she felt?" he asks, referring to Lannette.

"It don't matter anymore. Her actions have said enough for me."

As I begin to ride off, Harry pulls up behind me in his truck, gets out, and really starts showing his stupidity. "Get the fuck off my block!" he shouts. "I don't want to see your ass nowhere around here."

"Harry, is it really that serious?"

Clarence looks at me one last time and begins to walk away again. As I'm slowly pulling off, Harry continues on his rant about me being a Muskegon nigga, how he don't like Muskegon niggas, how he had to tell his boys not to come over his house to jack me up, and all this bullshit.

"I don't want to catch your ass in Benton Harbor city limits again." That's the last thing I hear him shout. He has taken it too far. Is it because I'm from Muskegon or he just didn't like me from jump? Whatever the case, I leave in one piece because it could have gotten ugly if I didn't keep my cool. Harry just showed his true colors and that he didn't like me because of his stereotype of me.

The next day on Christmas Eve, I call Shannel and tell her what went down, and she isn't surprised at all. She can't understand why he reacted the way he did, but she said I was smart for leaving and not taking it further than I did. To piss him off more, I send Harry a card apologizing. I want to know what type of level he's on from his response, if there is one. All in all, I was still shaken up by it all. I Invited my whole family over for Christmas dinner. My nieces, nephews, and cousins; our house was packed. I was in my room the whole time. Since the incident, I can't eat or sleep, and all I do is listen to Brian McKnight over and over again. I have lost the battle that I never had the chance of winning. I know now that everything will pretty much be history. I pray that Lannette will find enough courage and love in her heart to call me and tell me something. I want to at least know if Demond liked his gift I had gotten him. My mom came and checked on me to see if I was okay. She told me to eat something and to come communicate with the family. I didn't want anyone to see me in such a bad state of being, so I just stayed in my room. I contemplated how Lannette and Clarence were together and how stupid she made me look. Did I fall in love with a whore and who did I really fall in love with that summer weekend in May? I thought about not wanting to start over meeting someone else, falling in love, and the same thing happening again.

I was hurting and needing someone to talk to before I did something I didn't want to. At one point I thought about suicide or popping a whole bunch of pills. I couldn't go through with it though because God will never forgive me for that. I just have to deal with it. I understand that everything happens for a reason. I lost a good 10 pounds from not eating and not sleeping. When the weekend came around, I finally got an appetite but not a big one. Jeff talked me into going out with him and his friends to the same club that I met Lannette. I gave it some thought, and I wasn't going to let her mistake ruin my life. I was feeling better, but I wasn't over Lannette, and it hasn’t been easy to take my mind off her. I went around town looking for a bottle of Dom P. It was $100 a bottle but I didn't care though. I wanted to drink away the pain just like the song by Mobb Deep talks about.

On the way to the club in Grand Rapids, my brother is driving; his two friends are also with us and they are all trying to boost me up as I kill the bottle of Dom in the backseat. They are telling me not to sweat the situation and that eventually Lannette will realize what she lost. I keep taking the Dom P to the head and listening to the music playing as they keep talking. Jeff made a point that as long as Lannette has a baby's daddy, he’s entitled to see her because of them having that child together. It made me take the damn Dom P to the head even more. I was tired of thinking about her, but she was all I could think about. My brother and his friends tried to boost me up all they could though. One of his friends is going away to school in Minnesota real soon. Architecture is his thing—the boy can draw his ass off. He tells me everything happens for the best and now I can continue working on something that I want to do in my life. I remember sending him some demo tapes of me and my friend T rapping and trying to get it played on the radio. I tell him I had the desire to act, direct movies, and write plays. He told me to focus on that because I was too young to let the situation hold me back. He was right; I saw the clear picture that he was trying to get me to see. He also said that I have a lot going for myself by working and taking my time on figuring out what I really want to do with my life. “Don't let time get the best of you and everything will fall in perspective in due time.”

I was a little more at ease when we made it to the club, but I was still thinking about Lannette, especially when we got into the club. I begin to have flashbacks to when I first saw her and Shannel here. I go to the bar and I get a double shot of Remy to ease my mind a little more. By the time the club is over, I can hardly walk straight. I’m not feeling good and Lannette is on my mind until we get back to Muskegon. My buzz wears off and reality sets back in, which makes it worse. *I’ve lost her,* I think to myself. I did everything right and everything ended up going wrong. Things fall apart, but I never thought it would fall apart this fast.

After the weekend, we go back to work getting ready for the New Year's vacation. I still wasn't talking to anyone. I can't take it anymore, and people begin to notice that something is going on with me. Nick is the only person I trust there so I finally tell him what is wrong. He had figured out already that I was going through something with Lannette by the way I was acting. He broke it down to me as plain as day. "It's better to have loved and lost than to never have loved at all."

Nick also reminds me that life goes on, adding that she will realize in the long run what she had and eventually call me back. He also tells me that I need to be with a more mature, career-minded woman, but until then, life goes on and just forget about Lannette. "It's her loss."

I try to take these words of advice to heart, but it isn't that easy. On New Year's Eve, Lannette calls me but she says Demond wants to talk to me. He wanted to thank me for the bike I got him for Christmas. Lannette was too afraid to say anything to me, so after I talk to Demond, she hangs up the phone. That hurt. She could at least apologize for leaving me out there with Harry and having to deal with that big blowup. She at least owes me an explanation or something. She was treating me like she never loved me at all. I put my heart into everything, and I didn't take anything for granted. I truly loved Lannette and would have given anything to keep her happy. I cry anytime I think about the fun we used to have, but it's all memories now, and I dread this happening. It always happens to the good men and that's why the good men become dogs. No matter what, I'm not going to fall into that trap again. I'll just be more careful next time, I guess. I don't know very much, but I do know that I will never be the same.

After New Year's, I began to try to pick myself back up, but I'm not nearly over her. I have a talk with one of my closest friends from elementary school named Ron. He is the same age as me, but when it came to women, he knew and understood them. He wasn't even the type to have a lot of women. He has been with the same girl since high school. I guess him and his girl have a better understanding of their relationship; she doesn't have a baby daddy either. He gave me the best advice ever. He told me that it takes a fool to learn that love don't love anybody. It's the person who loves, it's the person who cares, it's the person. The person must love his or herself in order to have love for another. It made sense. Lannette didn't love herself because if she did she wouldn't have let Clarence get the best of her, doing the things he did to her. I don't want to believe that she used me to get back at Clarence, but what's done is done. It's a bitch when it's done to you.

A week and a half after New Year's, I called Lannette because I still want an explanation from her about the last incident that happened. She goes off on me, talking about she's a grown woman and she can be with whoever since her and I are not together anymore. I ask her if she ever loved me, even a little or not at all. She responds, “I loved you that much to let you go because I wasn't worthy of having you.”

“That’s a cop out. Just admit that you used me.”

Lannette never does. She says that she did love me, but she just wasn't the right woman for me. I knew after me that she would probably end back up with Clarence. I tell her I hope that she has a happy life with him. “All he wants to do is fuck you, because he damn sure doesn’t love you,” I say to her. “If he really loves you, he wouldn't have never done the things to you that he's done.”

She is the mother of his child, then he had a baby with someone else. Lannette was worth more than any amount of money. She should have been his Earth, his foundation, and he should have handled her with care like he would his own life. What Clarence don't realize is that having a child together doesn't mean that they should be together. If that's the case, he should be with his other baby's mother too huh? All in all, they're both confused, so they both deserve each other. After my talk with Lannette, I am still upset. I tried to get closure about the end of our relationship by getting her to admit that she used me, but she never admits it. But I already knew the answer.

When I go back to work, I'm joking and laughing again. I'm not going to let this ruin my life, and by God's grace I will have more glorious days to come. If nothing else, I have the memories that we shared and I'm glad I went through it now than later or not going through it at all. After work, I go to the gym to work out and shoot a little hoops to get back into the swing of things. After showering, I go home and begin preparing for bed. I turn on the TV and begin to watch Sports Center. They have Michael Jordan and his wife on, and he has announced his retirement. After hard work and discipline, Michael Jordan has accomplished a lot for himself. He has six NBA championships, endorsements up the ass, his own shoe, his own cologne, and plenty of money to burn. The best thing of all, and the most important thing I notice, is that he has a beautiful and strong-minded woman with him by his side and a family. That's something I hope to accomplish at one point in my lifetime before I leave this world. I thought Lannette was the only woman that I wanted to share that with. I know it's not easy for Jordan to let go of something that you love so much, put his heart into, and prayed for. Hard work and staying focused paid off for him. I know it won't be easy for me to let go, just like I'm far from wanting to let her go. I can't make her love me; I can't make her be with me. I continue to watch Jordan on SportsCenter as he begins to get emotional. I can see that it is very difficult for him to let go of something that is so important. Whether it's sports, a person, dog, or cat. When you truly love that person, sport, dog, or cat, it hurts when the love that you give is taken for granted. I don't even like the Chicago Bulls and them winning all those damn championships, but they worked hard for it and they deserve everything that they had coming. I deserve everything that I have coming to me, but I guess I don't deserve that. I suppose my heavenly father has other ideas for a brotha' like myself. The love that I had for Lannette will always be a beautiful thing. I never felt like that and she was a first real love. It's similar to Michael Jordan's love for basketball. The word "love" can be risky and it's so easy to say, but it's difficult to do and show for some people. For me, that is all I did-show love; nothing more, nothing less. It's as simple as 1, 2, 3 – as long as it comes from the heart. I'm pretty sure down the road I'll meet someone who I'm attracted to physically as well as mentally to love again. I'm pretty sure it won't be that simple for me, and that it is pretty fucked up to have to be like that, but when a person breaks your heart you're cautious of the past repeating itself.

As Jordan answers his final questions from the press, they begin to show his most memorable moments and accomplishments in basketball. All the game-winning shots, all the hard work, and championships he has won. It shows when his father was there with him and now his retirement. This is a very emotional time for him, and me too. As they show the final clips of his games, they begin to play Lauryn Hill's song "The Sweetest Thing". Yes it is a sweetest thing to love and know that your love is so real, so true, for one special someone that deserves it. Tears begin to roll down from my eyes as I watch the clips and listen to the song. Just like Michael Jordan and I are sharing the same pain, letting go of something or someone that you love so dearly and truly. He loves basketball but basketball didn't love him. His love for the sport got him those championships. When you love something, you have to show that love. That's all the proof in the world that you mean it. Saying it is just saying it, but where's the truth behind it? It's like Gotti loving the mob, the lights, and the cameras. When he got locked up, the cameras weren't around anymore. They love getting the stories behind him being who he was and getting the job done. After John Gotti was indicted, that one camera wasn’t around anymore. That's why it takes a fool to learn that love don't love nobody.

Made in the USA
Monee, IL
18 August 2021

74925681R00144